This book belongs to

Rex Smedvig

May 30, 1994

Love
   mom!

Favorite Tales From
HANS CHRISTIAN ANDERSEN

Edited by NANCY CHRISTENSEN HALL/Illustrated by CAROLYN EWING

Checkerboard Press, New York

For Katrina

Designed by Antler & Baldwin, Inc.

Copyright © 1988 Checkerboard Press, Inc.
30 Vesey Street, New York, New York 10007

Library of Congress Catalog Card Number: 87-63491   ISBN: 1-56288-253-8
Printed in the United States of America   0 9 8 7 6 5 4 3 2

Contents

The Little Mermaid

Far out in the ocean the water is as blue as the prettiest cornflower and as clear as crystal. It also is very, very deep. In fact, the bottom is far deeper than any anchor could ever reach. Beautiful flowers and plants grow there, and fishes, both large and small, glide between their swaying stems.

In the deepest spot of all once stood the castle of the Sea King. Its walls were built of coral, and its roof was formed of shells. In each shell was a glittering pearl.

The Sea King's wife had died many years before, and so his aged mother lived with him and helped care for the little sea princesses, her granddaughters. There were six beautiful children, the youngest the prettiest of them all. Her skin was as clear and delicate as a rose petal, and her eyes were as blue as the sea. Like the others, instead of feet, the little princess's body ended in a fish's tail.

Outside the castle was a beautiful garden in which trees grew with red and blue blossoms like flames of fire. The fruit on the trees glittered like gold, and the flowers and stems waved to and fro continuously. In the garden was a marble statue that had fallen to the bottom of the sea from a boat that was wrecked in a storm. It was a statue of a handsome boy, carved out of pure white stone. Nothing gave the youngest princess more pleasure than to sit and gaze upon it.

The little one loved to hear about the world above the sea. She made her grandmother tell her all she knew of the ships and the towns, the people and the forest animals. Her grandmother called the birds *fishes* so the child could understand what they were, for she had never seen birds, nor even the skies in which they flew.

"When you reach your fifteenth year," her grandmother told her, "you may rise up out of the sea and sit on the rocks in the moonlight and watch the great ships sail by. And you will also see the forests and towns."

The following year, the eldest sister would be fifteen. Since each princess was a year younger than the next, the youngest would have six years to wait before her turn came. None of them longed for her turn as much as she.

When the eldest was fifteen, she rose to the surface of the ocean. When she returned, she talked of the wonderful things she had seen. The most beautiful, she said, was to lie in the moonlight on a sandbank near the coast and gaze at a large town nearby. She told how the lights in the windows twinkled like hundreds of stars. She talked of the sound of music, the noise of carriages, the voices of human beings, and the merry peal of bells ringing in the steeples of churches.

The youngest sister listened to every word. Afterward, when she stood at the open window looking up through the dark blue water, she thought of the great city and imagined, even in the depths of the sea, she could hear the sound of the church bells.

The following year the second sister was given permission to rise to the surface of the water. She rose just as the sun was setting, and this, she said, was the most beautiful sight of all. The sky turned golden in color, and violet and rose-colored clouds floated above her. Amid the clouds flew a large flock of wild swans.

The third sister's turn was next. She was the boldest of them all, and she swam up a broad river that emptied itself into the sea. Beyond the banks she saw hills covered with beautiful vines. Palaces and castles peeped out from amid the proud trees of the forest. She heard the birds singing, and the rays of the sun were so powerful that she had to dive down under the water to cool her burning face. In a narrow creek she found a troop of children splashing in the water. She said she would never forget the beautiful forest, the green hills, and the pretty little children who could swim in the water, even without tails to help them.

The fourth sister was more timid. She remained in the midst of the sea, but she said it was quite as beautiful there as nearer to land. She had seen ships, but at such a great distance they looked like sea gulls. The dolphins had sported in the waves, and the great whales spouted water until it seemed as if a hundred fountains were shooting up in every direction.

The fifth sister's birthday fell in the winter, so she saw what the others had not seen when they first went to the surface. The sea looked quite green, and large icebergs were floating about. They were of wonderful shapes and glittered like diamonds. She had seated herself upon one of the largest, while the cold wind played with her hair. She told the others that all the ships had sailed by quickly, steering far away from the icebergs, as if they were afraid. Toward evening, as the sun went down, dark clouds covered the sky, thunder rolled, and lightning flashed. The red light of the setting sun glowed on the icebergs as they rocked and tossed on the heaving sea.

When the sisters were first allowed to rise to the surface, they were delighted with the new and beautiful sights they saw. But now, because they could go whenever they pleased, they had become indifferent. They decided it was far more beautiful down below, and more pleasant to be at home.

Yet still, in the evening hours, the five sisters would sometimes twine their arms around each other and rise to the surface in a row. Their voices were more beautiful than those of any human being, and before the approach of a storm, when they expected a ship would be lost, they swam before the vessel, singing sweetly of the delights to be found in the depths of the sea. But the sailors could not understand the mermaids' song. They thought it was just the howling of the storm. The depths of the sea could never be beautiful for them. If their ship sank, the men would be drowned, and only their dead bodies would reach the palace of the Sea King.

When the sisters rose arm in arm through the water in this way, their youngest sister would stand alone, looking after them, ready to cry, except that mermaids have no tears, and therefore, they suffer more.

At last the youngest princess reached her fifteenth year. "Now you are grown up," said her grandmother. "I will adorn you as I did your sisters." And she placed a wreath of white blossoms in her hair. In every flower was a pearl.

"Farewell," said the little princess, and she rose as lightly as a bubble to the surface of the water. The sun had just set as she raised her head above the waves. The clouds were tinted with crimson and gold, and through the glimmering twilight shone the evening star in all its beauty. The sea was calm, and the air was mild and fresh. She saw a large ship on the water. There was music and singing on board, and as darkness came a hundred colored lanterns were lighted.

The little mermaid swam close to the cabin windows, and now and then, as the waves lifted her up, she could look in through the clear glass window-panes and see the people within. Among them was a handsome young prince with large black eyes. He was sixteen years old, and his birthday was being celebrated with much rejoicing.

When the prince came out of the cabin, more than a hundred rockets rose in the sky, making it as bright as day. Then it appeared as if all the stars in heaven were falling. The little mermaid was startled. She had never seen fire-works before. But more wonderful to watch was the face of the young prince, who stood smiling while the music echoed through the clear night air.

It grew very late, yet the little mermaid could not take her eyes from the ship, or from the beautiful prince. The colored lanterns had been put out. No more rockets rose in the air. The music and singing had ceased. The sea became restless, and a moaning, grumbling sound could be heard beneath the waves. But still the little mermaid remained by the cabin window.

After a while the waves rose higher, clouds darkened the sky, and lightning appeared in the distance. A dreadful storm was approaching. The waves rose as high as mountains, as if they would overtop the mast, but the ship dived like a swan between them and then rose again on their lofty, foaming crests. To the little mermaid this was pleasant sport; not so to the sailors.

The ship groaned and creaked under the lashing of the sea as the waves broke over the deck, and the thick planks began to give way. The mainmast snapped, and the ship lay on its side with the water rushing in. Now the little mermaid knew that the crew was in danger. Even she had to be careful to avoid the beams and planks of the wreck that tossed upon the water. One moment it was so dark that she could not see a single object, then a flash of lightning revealed the whole scene. Now she could see everyone who had been on board, except the prince. When the ship broke, she had seen him sink into the deep waves and, for a moment, she was glad, for she thought he would now be with her. Then she remembered that human beings could not live in the water, so that when he got down to her father's palace, he would be dead.

She swam among the beams and planks that floated on the sea, without a thought that they could crush her. Then she dived deep under the dark waters, where at last she found the young prince, who was struggling in the stormy sea. His arms and legs were failing him. His beautiful eyes were closed. He would surely have died had not the little mermaid come to his assistance. She brought him to the surface and held his head above the water, letting the waves carry them where they would.

By morning the storm had ceased. Not a single fragment of the ship could be seen. The sun rose red and glowing from the water, and its rays returned the hue of health to the prince's cheeks. But his eyes remained closed. The mermaid kissed his high, smooth forehead and stroked his wet hair. He seemed to her like the marble statue in her garden, and she wished that he might live.

13

Presently they came in sight of land. In the distance rose lofty blue mountains. Near the coast grew beautiful green forests, and close by stood a large building that looked like a church or a convent. The sea here formed a little bay in which the water was quite still, but very deep. So the little princess swam with the handsome prince to the beach, which was covered with fine white sand. There she laid him in the warm sunshine.

The bells sounded in the large white building, and several young girls came into the garden. The little mermaid swam away from the shore and hid between some rocks that rose up out of the water. She covered her head and neck with the foam of the sea to hide her little face, and she watched to see what would become of the prince. She had not waited long before a young girl approached the spot where he lay. The girl seemed frightened at first, but only for a moment. Then she fetched a number of people, and the mermaid saw the prince come to life again and smile at those who stood around him.

But to the little mermaid he sent no smile. He did not know that she had saved him. This made her very sad, and when he was led away into the great building, she dived down into the water and returned to her father's castle.

The little mermaid had always been silent and thoughtful, and now she became more so than ever. Her sisters asked what she had seen during her first visit to the surface of the water, but she would tell them nothing. On many a morning and evening she rose to the place where she had left the prince. She saw the fruits in the garden ripen. She saw the snow on the tops of the mountains melt away. But she never saw the prince. Each time she returned home, she was more sorrowful than before. Her only comfort was to sit in the garden and gaze at the marble statue that looked like the prince. At last she could bear her sorrow no longer, and she told one of her sisters what had happened. Then the others heard the secret, and very soon a mermaid who had also seen the festival on the prince's ship told them how to find the place where the prince's palace stood.

"Come, little sister," said the other princesses. Then they entwined their arms and rose up in a row to the surface of the water, close to the place where they knew the prince's palace to be. It was a splendid castle, and through the clear crystal of the lofty windows they saw noble rooms with curtains of silk and hangings of tapestry.

Now that she knew where the prince lived, the little mermaid spent many an evening in the water near the palace. She would swim much nearer to the shore than any of her sisters dared. Here she would sit and watch the young prince, who believed himself quite alone.

On many a night, too, when the fishermen were out to sea, she heard them say good things about the young prince, and she was glad she had saved his life. The little mermaid grew more and more fond of human beings, and soon she wished to be able to fly over the sea in ships and climb the high mountains that rose far above the clouds. She longed to see the woods and the fields that stretched far beyond the reach of her sight.

There was so much that she wished to know, but her sisters were unable to answer all her questions. So she turned to her old grandmother, who knew most about the world above the sea. "If human beings are not drowned," asked the little mermaid, "can they live forever? Do they never die as we do here in the sea?"

"No," replied the old lady, "they too must die, and their lives are much shorter than our own. We sometimes live to three hundred years, but when we die, we become foam on the surface of the water. We do not have immortal souls. Human beings have souls that live after their bodies have turned to dust. Their souls rise up through the clear, pure air beyond the glittering stars. As we rise out of the water and behold the earth, they rise to unknown and glorious places that we shall never see."

"Why do we not have immortal souls?" asked the little mermaid. "I would give up all the hundreds of years I have to live to gain a soul and be a human being for only one day. But instead I shall die and become the foam of the sea. Is there nothing I can do to win an immortal soul?" she asked sadly.

"No," said the old woman, "unless a human being loved you so much that you were more precious to him than his father or mother. All his thoughts and all his love would have to be fixed upon you, and he would have to take you for his bride. Only then would his soul glide into your body, and you would obtain a share in the happiness of mankind. He would give a soul to you and retain his own as well. But this can never happen. Your fish's tail, which we consider so beautiful, is thought on earth to be quite ugly. People believe it is necessary to have two stout props, which they call legs, in order to be handsome."

Then the little mermaid sighed and looked sorrowfully at her fish's tail. "Let us be happy," said the old lady, "and dart and swim about during the three hundred years that we have to live, which is really quite long enough. Let us end this talk of death and immortal souls," she said, "for this evening we are going to have a ball. We have so much for which we should be grateful."

The ball at the bottom of the sea was a splendid sight. The walls and the ceiling of the large ballroom were made of crystal. Hundreds of shells holding blue fire torches stood in rows on each side to light the room. Through the halls flowed a broad stream, and in it danced the mermen and mermaids to the music of their own sweet singing. No one on earth has a voice more lovely than a mermaid's, and the little mermaid sang most sweetly of them all.

At first the little mermaid was happy, but soon her thoughts turned back to the world above her. She could not forget her charming prince, nor her sorrow that she did not have an immortal soul. So she crept away silently from her father's palace, and while everything within was gladness and song, she sat in the garden, sorrowful and alone.

The little mermaid knew that she would give up everything she had to win the love of the prince and to gain an immortal soul. While her sisters were dancing in her father's palace, she decided to visit the Sea Witch, of whom she had always been very much afraid. She knew that the Sea Witch would know just what she must do.

The little mermaid began the journey on the road to the foaming whirlpools behind which the sorceress lived. She had never been that way before. Neither flowers nor grass grew there. There was nothing but bare, gray sand stretching out to the whirlpools, where the water, like foaming millwheels, whirled around everything that it seized and cast it into the fathomless deep.

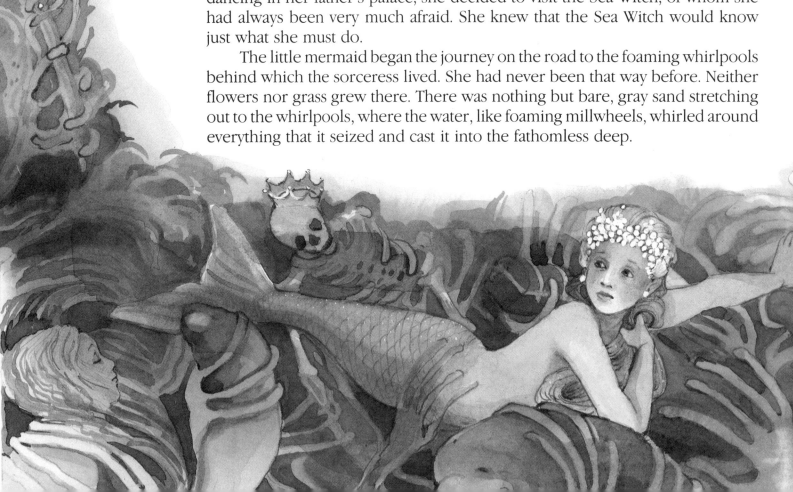

The little mermaid had to pass through the midst of these crushing whirl-pools. Beyond this, she came to a strange forest in which all the trees and flowers were half animals and half plants. These plants looked to her like serpents with a hundred heads growing out of the ground. Their branches were long slimy arms, with fingers like worms, moving limb after limb from their roots to their tops. Everything they could reach they grabbed and held fast, so that it never escaped from their clutches. There, in a marsh surrounded by these plants, stood the witch's house.

The little mermaid was so frightened by what she saw that she stood still, and her heart beat so with fear that she very nearly turned back. But then she thought of the prince, and the human soul for which she longed, and her courage returned. She fastened her long flowing hair around her head so that the plants might not grab hold of it. Then she darted forward between the ugly arms and fingers that stretched out on either side of her. She saw that each one held in its grasp something it had seized with its numerous little arms. She saw the white skeletons of human beings who had perished at sea and had sunk down into the deep waters. She saw chests from their ships, skeletons of animals, and most shocking of all to the little princess, she saw a little mermaid, whom they had caught in their clutches.

Finally she came to a space of marshy ground in the forest, where large, fat water snakes were rolling in the mire. In the midst of this spot stood a house built of bones. She heard the Sea Witch within call the ugly water snakes her little chickens, and she saw her let the water snakes crawl all over her body and eat from her plate.

"I know what you want," cackled the Sea Witch to the little mermaid. "It is very stupid of you, but you shall have your way, and it will bring you nothing but sorrow, my pretty princess. You want to get rid of your fish's tail and have two legs instead, like human beings on earth, so that the young prince will fall in love with you, and you may gain an immortal soul." And then the witch

laughed so loudly and disgustingly that the snakes fell to the ground and lay there wriggling about. "So I will prepare a potion for you. You must swim to land tomorrow before sunrise and sit down on the shore and drink it. Then your tail will disappear and change into what mankind calls legs, and you will feel great pain, as if a sword were passing through you. But all who see you will say that you are the prettiest little human they have ever seen. You will still have your gracefulness of movement, and no dancer will ever tread as lightly as you, but with every step you take, you will feel as if you were treading upon sharp knives. If you can bear all this, I will help you."

"Yes, I shall," said the little princess in a trembling voice, as she thought of marrying the prince and winning an immortal soul.

"But think again," said the witch. "For once your shape has changed, you can never again be a mermaid. You can never return through the water to see your sisters or visit your father's palace. And if the prince does not take you for his bride, you will not gain an immortal soul. The morning after he marries another, your heart will break, and you will become foam on the crest of the waves."

"I will do it," said the little mermaid softly, and she became as pale as death.

"Then I must be paid," said the witch, "and it is not a trifle that I ask. You have the sweetest voice of any who dwell in the depths of the sea. But you will not be able to charm your prince with it, for you must give your voice to me. I will have the best thing you possess for the price of my special potion."

"But if you take away my voice," said the little mermaid, "what is left for me?"

"Your beautiful smile, your graceful walk, and your expressive eyes. Surely with these you can enchain a man's heart. Have you lost your courage? Come, put out your tongue that I may cut it off as my payment."

"It shall be," said the little mermaid.

Then the witch placed her cauldron on the fire to prepare the magic potion. Next she pricked herself with a needle and let her black blood drop into it. The steam that rose formed itself into such horrible shapes that no one could have looked at them without fear. The witch threw many strange ingredients into the potion, and when it began to boil, the sound was like the weeping of a crocodile. When at last the magic drink was ready, it looked like the clearest spring water. "Here it is," said the witch, and she held out the potion to the princess.

The little mermaid passed quickly through the woods and marshes and between the rushing whirlpools. She saw that the torches in the ballroom were extinguished, and all within the castle were asleep. She did not stop, for now she had no voice and was leaving her family forever. She felt as if her heart would break.

She rose up through the dark blue waters. The sun had not yet risen when

she came in sight of the prince's palace. She approached the beautiful marble steps, and then the little mermaid drank the magic potion. It seemed as if a two-edged sword went through her delicate body. She fell into a swoon and lay as if dead. When the sun rose and shone over the sea, she recovered and felt a sharp pain. But before her stood the handsome young prince. He fixed his coal-black eyes upon her so earnestly that she cast down her own, and only then did she become aware that her fish's tail was gone. She had as pretty a pair of legs and tiny feet as any little maiden could have. But she had no clothes, so she wrapped herself in her long, thick hair.

The prince asked her who she was and where she had come from, and she looked at him sorrowfully with her deep blue eyes. She could not speak, and every step she took was as the witch had said it would be. She felt as if she were treading upon needle points or sharp knives; but she bore it willingly and stepped lightly by the prince's side. Soon she was arrayed in costly robes of silk and gold, and she was the most beautiful creature in the palace. But she could neither speak nor sing.

That evening she joined the prince for a banquet. Beautiful young women stepped forward and sang for the prince and his royal parents. One sang better than all the others, and the prince clapped his hands and smiled at her. This was a great sorrow to the little mermaid. She knew how much more sweetly she herself could once sing, and she thought, "If he could only know that I have given away my voice to be with him."

Next, the women danced to the beautiful music. Then the little mermaid raised her lovely white arms, stood on the tips of her toes, and glided across the floor, dancing as no one else was able to do. At each moment her beauty became more apparent. Everyone was enchanted, especially the prince, who

19

called her his little foundling. She danced again to please him, though each time her foot touched the floor, it felt as if she were stepping on sharp knives.

The prince asked her to remain with him always. They rode together through the sweet-scented woods. They climbed to the tops of high mountains, and although her tender feet bled when she walked, she only laughed, and followed him until they could see the clouds beneath them.

When everyone in the prince's palace was fast asleep, she would go and sit on the broad marble steps that led to the sea. It eased her burning feet to bathe them in the cold seawater, and she thought then of all those below in the deep. Once, during the night, her sisters came up arm in arm, singing sorrowfully as they floated on the water. She beckoned to them, and they recognized her and told her how they grieved for her. After that, they came to the same place every night. Once she saw her old grandmother in the distance, and another time she was sure she saw the Sea King himself.

As the days passed, she loved the prince still more, and he loved her as he would love a little child, but it never came into his head to make her his wife. Yet unless he married her, she could not gain an immortal soul, and on the morning after his marriage to another, she would dissolve into the foam of the sea.

"Do you not love me the best of all?" the eyes of the little mermaid seemed to ask when he took her in his arms.

"You are very dear to me," said the prince, "for you have the best heart, and you are the most devoted to me. You are like a young maiden whom I once saw, but whom I fear I shall never meet again. I was in a ship that was wrecked, and the waves cast me ashore near a holy temple where several young maidens were studying. The youngest of them found me on the beach and saved my life. I saw her just once, but I am sure that she is the only one in the world whom I can truly love. You are like her, and since you have come, she is much less on my mind."

"He does not know that it was I who saved his life," thought the little mermaid. "I carried him over the sea to the land where the temple stands. I sat beneath the foam and watched until the human beings came to help him. I saw the pretty maiden that he loves better than he loves me." The little mermaid sighed deeply, but she could not shed tears.

Very soon it was said that the prince must marry, and that the beautiful daughter of a neighboring king would be his wife. The prince agreed to pay a visit to the king, and it was generally assumed that he really wanted to see the daughter. A great party of courtiers was to accompany him.

"I must travel," the prince told the little mermaid. "My parents desire that I see this beautiful princess. But they will not force me to bring her home as my bride. I know I cannot love her. She is not the beautiful maiden in the temple whom you resemble. If I must choose a bride, I would rather choose you." And then he kissed her and played with her beautiful long hair, while she dreamed of human happiness and an immortal soul.

"You will come with me on my journey," the prince said. "Do not be afraid of the sea." And he told her of storms and of calm, of strange fishes, and of what the divers had seen. She smiled at his descriptions, for she knew better than anyone what wonders could be found at the bottom of the sea.

The next morning the ship sailed into the harbor of a beautiful town belonging to the king whom the prince was to visit. The church bells were ringing, and from the high towers a flourish of trumpets was heard. Soldiers with flying colors and glittering lances lined the streets. Every day following that there was a festival for the prince, with balls and entertainments one after another.

But the princess did not appear. People said that she was away being educated in a holy house where she was learning every royal virtue. When she finally came home, the little mermaid was obliged to acknowledge that she had never seen a human being more perfect than the princess. Her skin was delicately fair, and beneath her long dark eyelashes her laughing blue eyes shone with truth and purity.

"It was you," said the prince when he saw her. "You saved my life when I lay dying on the beach." And he took his bride-to-be in his arms. All the church

bells rang, and the heralds rode about the town proclaiming the betrothal. "Oh, I am too happy," he said to the little mermaid. "My fondest hopes are fulfilled. You must rejoice at my happiness, for your devotion to me is great and sincere."

The little mermaid kissed his hand, and felt as if her heart were breaking. His marriage would bring her death, and she would change into the foam of the sea.

The bride and bridegroom joined their hands and received the blessing of the bishop. The little mermaid, dressed in silk and gold, held up the bride's train, but her ears heard nothing of the festive music, and her eyes saw nothing of the holy ceremony. She thought only of the death that was coming to her, and of all she had lost in the world.

That very evening the bride and bridegroom went on board the prince's ship. Cannons were booming, flags were waving, and in the center of the ship a costly tent of purple and gold had been erected. The ship glided away smoothly and lightly over the calm sea. When it grew dark, colored lamps were lit, and the sailors danced merrily on the deck. The little mermaid could not help thinking of the first time she had risen out of the sea and seen similar festivities and joy.

She joined in the dancing, and everyone present looked upon her with

wonder. She had never before danced so beautifully. Although her tender feet felt as if they were cut with sharp knives, she cared not. A sharper pain had pierced through her heart. She knew this was the last evening she would ever see the prince, for whom she had forsaken her family and her home. She had given up her beautiful voice and suffered pain each day for him, while he knew nothing of it. This was the last evening that she would gaze upon the starry sky and the deep blue sea. She had no soul, and now she could never win one.

Aboard the ship all was joy and gaiety until long after midnight. The little mermaid laughed and danced with the rest, while thoughts of death were in her heart. The prince kissed his beautiful bride while she played with his raven hair. At last they went arm in arm to rest in the splendid tent. Then all became still on board the ship. Only the little mermaid remained on deck. She leaned her white arms on the edge of the vessel and looked toward the east for the first blush of morning, the first ray of dawn that would bring her death.

Just then she saw her sisters rising out of the water. They were as pale as she, and their long beautiful hair no longer waved in the wind. "We have given our hair to the witch," they said, "that you may not die this morning. She has given us a knife. It is very sharp. Before the sun rises, you must plunge this knife into the heart of the prince. When his warm blood falls upon your feet,

they will grow together again and form a fish's tail, and you will once more be a mermaid and return to us to live out your three hundred years. But hurry, for either he or you must die as the sun rises. Our old grandmother moans so for you that her white hair is falling out from sorrow, as ours fell under the witch's scissors. Kill the prince and come back. But hurry, for in a few minutes the sun will rise, and you will die." And then they sighed deeply and mournfully and sank beneath the waves.

The little mermaid drew back the curtain of the tent and beheld the fair bride with her head resting on the prince's breast. She bent down and kissed his brow, and then looked at the sky on which the rosy dawn grew brighter and brighter. She glanced at the sharp knife, then again fixed her eyes on the prince, who whispered the name of his beloved bride in his sleep.

The knife trembled in the hands of the little mermaid. She flung it far away into the waves. The water turned red where the knife fell, and the drops that spurted up looked like blood. She cast one more glance at the prince, and then threw herself from the ship into the sea and felt her body dissolving into foam. The sun rose above the waves, and its warm rays fell on the cold form of the little mermaid, who did not feel as if she were dying.

She saw the bright sun, and all around her floated hundreds of transparent beautiful beings. Through them she could see the white sails of the ship and the rosy clouds in the sky. The little mermaid saw that her body, too, was transparent, and that she was rising higher and higher out of the foam.

"Where am I?" she asked, and her voice sounded like the voices of those who were with her. No earthly music could imitate it.

"You are among the daughters of the air," one answered. "A mermaid does not have an immortal soul, nor can she obtain one unless she wins the love of a human. Her eternal destiny depends on the power of another. But, although the daughters of the air do not possess immortal souls, they can, by their good deeds, procure them. We fly to the very hot countries, where the stifling air means death to mankind, and we bring cool breezes. We carry the perfume of the flowers through the air and send comfort and healing. After we have striven for three hundred years to do all the good we can, we receive immortal souls and join in the happiness of mankind.

"You, little mermaid, have tried with your whole heart to do as we do. You have suffered and have endured and raised yourself by your good deeds. Now, by striving for three hundred years in the same way, you too may obtain an immortal soul."

The little mermaid lifted her eyes toward the sun and, for the first time, felt them fill with tears. On the ship where she had left the prince there was a great commotion. She saw the prince and his beautiful bride searching for her. Sorrowfully, they gazed at the pearly foam, as if they knew she had thrown herself into the waves. Unseen, she kissed the forehead of the bride and fanned the brow of the prince. Then she joined the other maidens of the air on a rosy cloud that floated through the sky. "After three hundred years, we shall gain immortal souls," she said aloud.

"We may even get there sooner," whispered one of her companions. "Unseen we can enter houses where there are children, and each time we find a child who is good, our time of trial is shortened. The child does not know that when we fly through the room, we smile with joy at good behavior, for then we can count one fewer year of our three hundred years. But when we see a naughty or wicked child, we shed tears of sorrow, and for every tear that falls, a day is added to our time of trial!"

The Ugly Duckling

It was a lovely summer day in the country. The golden corn, the green oats, and the haystacks in the meadows looked beautiful. The stork walked about on his long red legs chattering in Egyptian, a language he had learned from his mother.

In a sunny spot close to a deep river stood a pleasant old farmhouse. From the house down to the waterside great burdock leaves grew so high that a child could stand beneath them. In this snug retreat sat a duck on her nest, waiting for her young brood to hatch. She was beginning to get tired of her task, for the little ones were a long time coming out of their shells, and she seldom had any visitors.

The other ducks preferred swimming about in the river to climbing the slippery banks to sit under a burdock leaf and gossip with her. At last, one shell cracked, and then another. From each egg came a little duckling that lifted its head and cried, "Peep, peep!"

"Quack, quack," said the mother, and then all the ducklings quacked as well as they could. The little ducklings looked all around. They were delighted with what they saw, especially the big green leaves.

"How large the world is," they said when they found out how much more room they had now than while they were inside their eggshells.

"Do you think this is the whole world?" asked the mother. "Wait till you see the garden." But as she began to rise she noticed that the largest egg had not yet cracked. "I wonder how long this one is going to take," she said with a sigh, seating herself once again. "I am quite tired of sitting on this nest."

"Well, how are you getting on?" asked an old duck who was passing by.

"One egg has not yet hatched," said the mother duck. "But look what came out of all the others. Are they not the prettiest little ducklings you ever saw?"

"Let me see the egg that will not hatch," said the old duck. "I have no doubt it is a turkey's egg. I was persuaded to hatch some once, and after all my care and trouble with the young ones, they were afraid of the water. I quacked and clucked, but all to no purpose. I could not get them to venture in. Let me look at the egg. Yes, that is a turkey's egg. Take my advice. Leave it where it is, and teach the other children to swim."

"I think I will sit on it a little while longer," said the mother duck. "Since I have sat so long already, a few days more will not matter."

"Please yourself," said the old duck, and she waddled away.

At last the large egg broke, and a young bird crawled out crying, "Peep, peep!" It was much larger than the other ducklings and very ugly. The mother duck stared at it and exclaimed, "It is very large and not at all like the others. I wonder if it really is a turkey. We shall certainly find out soon enough."

The next day the weather was delightful. The mother duck led her young brood down to the water. She jumped in with a splash.

"Quack, quack!" she cried, and one after another, the little ducklings jumped in after her. They swam about prettily with their little legs paddling beneath them. The ugly duckling swam happily with the others.

"Well," said the mother, "he is not a turkey. How well he uses his legs, and how upright he holds himself! He is truly my own child, and he is not so very ugly after all. You just have to look at him properly. Quack, quack!" she called to her children. "Come with me now. I will take you to the farmyard. But you must keep close to me, or you may be trodden upon. And above all, beware of the cat."

When they reached the farmyard, the mother duck whispered, "Come, now, let me see how well you can behave. Be sure to bow your heads prettily to that old duck by the fence. She is the highest born of us all. Come, now, don't turn your toes. Well-bred ducklings' feet spread wide apart. Now bend your neck and say, 'quack.'"

The ducklings did as they were told. But one of the ducks in the farmyard stared at them and said to the others, "Look, here comes another brood, as if there were not enough of us already! And what a queer-looking object one of them is. We don't want *him* around here." Then she flew at the ugly duckling and bit him on the neck.

"Leave him alone," said the mother. "He is not doing any harm."

"Yes, but he is so big and ugly," said the spiteful duck.

"The others are pretty children," the old duck by the fence told the mother duck, "all but that one. I wish you could improve him a little."

"That is impossible," replied the mother. "I know he is not pretty, but he is very good, and he swims as well, or even better, than the others. Perhaps he will grow up pretty and not so large." Then she stroked his neck and smoothed

his feathers, saying, "I think he will grow up strong and able to take care of himself."

"Well, the other ducklings are graceful enough," said the old duck. "Now make yourselves at home."

And so they made themselves comfortable. But the poor duckling who had crept out of his shell last of all was not made to feel welcome. All the ducks and other animals in the farmyard made fun of him, and some even bit and pushed him.

Every day was the same. The poor duckling was badly treated by everyone. His brothers and sisters were unkind to him and would say, "Ah, you ugly creature, I wish the cat would get you," until even his own mother said she wished he had never been born. The ducks pecked him. The chickens chased him. The girl who fed them kicked him with her feet.

At last the ugly duckling felt so unhappy he decided to run away. He went as far as he could until, at last, he came to a large moor inhabited by wild ducks. Here he remained the whole night, feeling very tired and sorrowful.

In the morning, when the wild ducks rose into the air, they stared at their new comrade. "What sort of a duck are you?" they all asked, crowding around him.

He bowed to them and was as polite as he could be, but he did not know the answer to their question. "You are exceedingly ugly," said the wild ducks, "but that does not matter, provided you do not want to marry anyone in our family."

Poor thing! He had no thoughts of marriage. All he wanted was to rest peacefully among the rushes and drink some of the water on the moor.

After the ugly duckling had been on the moor two days, two wild geese, or rather goslings, for they had not been out of their eggs for long, came to talk to him.

"Listen, friend," said one of them to the duckling, "you are very ugly, but we like you very well. Not far from here is another moor where we would like to visit. Will you come with us?"

The little duckling was so happy to finally have friends. But suddenly a popping noise sounded in the air. The two wild geese fell dead among the rushes, and the water was tinged with blood. "Pop, pop," echoed far and wide in the distance. Whole flocks of wild geese rose up from the rushes.

The sound continued from every direction, for hunters surrounded the moor. The blue smoke from their guns rose like clouds over the dark trees. As it floated away across the water, a number of dogs bounded in among the rushes. How they terrified the poor duckling! He turned his head to hide it under his wing. At that very moment a large terrible dog passed quite near him. Its jaws were open, and its tongue hung out of its mouth. The dog thrust its nose close to the duckling, showing its sharp teeth. Then it splashed away into the water without touching him.

"Oh," said the poor little duckling, "how thankful I am for being so ugly. Even a dog will not bite me." And so he lay still, while the shots rattled through the rushes. Gun after gun was fired over him.

It was late in the day before the poor young thing dared to move. After looking carefully around him, he hurried away from the moor as fast as he could. He ran over fields and meadows until a storm arose. He could hardly struggle against it.

Toward evening he reached a little cottage that only remained standing because it could not decide which way to fall. The storm raged so violently that the duckling could go no farther. He sat down by the cottage door. Then he noticed that one of the hinges had given way, and the door was not quite closed. There was a narrow opening near the bottom just large enough for him to slip through. This he did very quietly, and so he found shelter for the night.

A woman, a tomcat, and a hen lived in the cottage. The tomcat, whom the woman called "My Little Son," was a great favorite. He could raise his back and purr. He could even throw out sparks from his fur if it was stroked the wrong way. The hen had very short legs, so she was called "Chickie Short Legs." She laid good eggs, and her mistress loved her dearly.

In the morning, the strange visitor was discovered, and the tomcat began to purr and Chickie Short Legs to cluck.

"What is that noise about?" asked the old woman, whose sight was not very good. She looked around the room. When she saw the duckling, she exclaimed, "A big, fat duck! What a prize! I hope it is not a drake, for if it is not, I shall have some duck's eggs. I must wait and see." So the duckling was allowed to remain for three weeks, at the end of which there were no eggs.

One day, as the sunshine and the fresh air came into the room through the open door, the duckling began to feel a great longing for a swim. He could not help telling the hen.

"What an absurd idea," said the hen. "You have nothing else to do, and therefore you have foolish thoughts. If you could purr or lay eggs, your fancies would pass."

"But swimming is so delightful," said the duckling, "and it is so refreshing to feel the water close over your head when you dive down to the bottom."

"Delightful, indeed!" said the hen. "Why, you must be crazy! Ask the cat. He is the cleverest animal I know. Ask him how he would like to swim about in the water, or to dive under it, for I will not speak of my own opinion. Ask our mistress, the old woman. There is no one in the world more clever than she. Do you think she would like to go for a swim, or to let the water close over her head?"

"You don't understand me," said the duckling.

"We don't understand you? Who can understand you, I wonder. Do you consider yourself more clever than the cat or the old woman? I will say nothing of myself. Don't imagine such nonsense, and thank your good fortune that you

31

are in a warm room and in company from which you may learn something. I advise you to lay eggs and learn to purr as quickly as possible."

"I believe I must go out into the world again," said the duckling.

"Then do," said the hen.

So the duckling left the cottage and soon found water in which he could swim and dive. But still he had no friends because of his ugly appearance. Autumn came, and the leaves in the forest turned to orange and gold. Then, as winter approached, the wind caught them and whirled them in the cold air. The clouds, heavy with hail and snowflakes, hung low in the sky. The raven stood on the ferns crying, "Croak, croak." It made one shiver with cold to look at him.

All this was very sad for the poor little duckling. One evening, just as the sun was setting amidst radiant clouds, a large flock of beautiful birds came out of the bushes. The duckling had never seen any like them before. They were swans. They curved their graceful necks, while their soft plumage shone with dazzling whiteness. They uttered a singular cry as they spread their glorious wings and prepared to fly away from those cold regions to warmer countries far across the sea.

The swans rose higher and higher in the air. The ugly little duckling felt a strange sensation as he watched them. He whirled himself in the water like a wheel and stretched out his neck toward them. He uttered a cry so strange that it frightened him. When at last they were out of sight, he dived under the water, and rose again almost beside himself with excitement. He did not know the name of these birds, nor where they had flown, but he felt toward them as he had never felt toward any other bird in the world. He was not envious of these beautiful creatures, but he wished he were as lovely as they. Poor ugly creature.

The winter grew colder and colder. Every night the space in which he swam became smaller and smaller. The duckling had to paddle with all his might to keep the space from closing up. At last the pond froze so hard that the ice in the water crackled as he moved. He became exhausted and lay still and helpless, frozen fast in the ice.

Early in the morning a peasant who was passing by saw what had happened. He broke the ice with his wooden shoe and carried the duckling home to his wife. The warmth in the kitchen revived the poor little creature. But when the children wanted to play with him, the duckling thought they would hurt him, so he started up in terror, fluttered into the milk pan, and splashed the milk about the room. Then the woman clapped her hands, which frightened him still more. He flew first into the barrel filled with butter. Then he flew into the meal tub and out again.

What a state he was in! The woman screamed and struck at him with tongs. The children laughed and tumbled over each other trying to catch him. The door stood open and luckily he escaped. The poor duckling crawled out among the bushes and lay down quite exhausted in the newly fallen snow.

It would be very sad to relate all the misery that the poor little duckling endured during that hard winter. But in time it passed, and one morning he found himself lying among the rushes in a moor. He felt the warm sun shining and heard the lark singing. He saw that spring had finally come.

The young bird felt that his wings were strong. He flapped them against his sides and rose high into the air. They bore him onward until, before he knew what had happened, he found himself in a large garden. The apple trees were in full blossom. The fragrant elders bent their long green branches down to the stream that wound around a smooth lawn. Everything looked beautiful in the freshness of early spring.

33

From a thicket close by came three beautiful white swans, rustling their feathers and swimming lightly over the smooth water. The duckling remembered the lovely birds, and he felt more strangely unhappy than ever.

"I will fly to those royal birds," he exclaimed, "and they will kill me because I am so ugly and dare to approach them. But it does not matter. It is better to be killed by them than pecked by the ducks, bitten by the hens, pushed about by the maiden who feeds the poultry, or starved with hunger in the winter."

So he flew to the water and swam toward the beautiful swans. The moment they spied the stranger, they rushed to meet him with outstretched wings.

"Kill me," said the poor bird. He bent his head down to the surface of the water and awaited death.

But what did he see in the clear stream below? His own image. He was no longer a dark gray bird, ugly and disagreeable to look at. He was a graceful and beautiful swan. To be born in a duck's nest is of no consequence to a bird, if it is hatched from a swan's egg.

He now felt glad at having suffered sorrow and trouble, because it enabled him to enjoy so much better all the pleasure and happiness around him. The

great swans swam around the newcomer and stroked his neck with their beaks to welcome him.

Just then, some little children came into the garden, throwing bread and cake into the water.

"See," cried the youngest, "there is a new one." The others were delighted and ran to tell their mother and father. Joyously they shouted, "Another swan has come. A new one has arrived."

Then they threw more bread and cake into the water and said, "The new one is the most beautiful of all. He is so young and pretty." And the old swans bowed their heads before him.

Then he hid his head under his wing. He did not know what to do. He was so happy, and yet not at all proud. He had been persecuted and despised for his ugliness, and now he heard them say he was the most beautiful of all the birds. Even the elder tree bent down its bows into the water before him, and the sun shone warm and bright. Then he rustled his feathers, curved his slender neck, and from the depths of his heart joyfully cried, "I never dreamed of such happiness as this while I was an ugly duckling."

The Steadfast Tin Soldier

here were once twenty-five tin soldiers who were all brothers, for they had all been made out of the same old tin spoon. They carried rifles and looked straight before them. Each wore a splendid uniform of red, white, and blue.

The first thing in the world they ever heard were the words, "Tin soldiers!" which were uttered by a little boy, who clapped his hands with delight when the lid was taken off the box in which they lay.

The soldiers had been given to him as a birthday present, and he stood at the table to set them up. Each was exactly alike, except one, who had only one leg. This soldier had been the last to be made, and there was not enough of the melted tin to finish him. So he was made to stand firmly on just one leg, and this caused him to be very remarkable.

On the table where the tin soldiers stood were other playthings. The nicest of all was a pretty little paper castle. In front of the castle a number of little trees surrounded a piece of mirror, which was intended to look like a lake. Swans made of wax swam on the lake and were reflected in it.

All this was very pretty, but the prettiest of all was a tiny little lady who stood at the open door of the castle. She was also made of paper, and she wore a dress of muslin with a narrow blue ribbon over her shoulders like a scarf. In front of the ribbon was a glittering tinsel rose. The little lady was a dancer. She stretched out both of her arms and raised one of her legs so high that the tin soldier could not see it at all. And that is why he thought that she, like himself, had only one leg.

36

"That is the wife for me," he thought. "But she is so grand, and she lives in a castle, while I have only a box to live in, twenty-five of us together. That is no place for her. Still I must try and make her acquaintance."

Then he hid behind a small box on the table, so that he could peep at the lovely lady who continued to stand on one leg without losing her balance. When evening came, the twenty-four other tin soldiers were placed in their box, and the people of the house went to bed.

Then all of the playthings that remained on the table began to play games and visit one another. They even had a wonderful party with dancing and music.

The tin soldiers rattled in their box. They wanted to join the fun, but they could not get out. The nutcrackers played leapfrog. The pencil jumped about on the table. There was such a noise that the canary woke up and began to talk in poetry!

Only the tin soldier and the dancer remained in their places, each firmly supported by just one leg. He never took his eyes from her, not even for a moment.

When the clock struck twelve, up sprang the lid of the box and out jumped a little goblin, for the box was a toy box, as it turned out.

"Tin soldier," said the goblin, "don't wish for what does not belong to you."

But the tin soldier pretended not to hear.

"Very well, then, wait till tomorrow," said the goblin.

When the children came in the next morning, they placed the tin soldier on the windowsill. Now, whether it was the goblin who did it, or the wind, it is not known, but the window flew open, and out fell the tin soldier into the street below. It was a terrible fall, for he went head downward for three stories. His helmet and bayonet stuck between two flagstones, and his one leg stuck straight up in the air.

The maidservant and the little boy ran downstairs at once to look for him, but the tin soldier was nowhere to be seen. Once they came so close that they nearly stepped on him, but then they passed him by. If he could have shouted, "Here I am," it would have been all right, but he was too proud to call for help while he wore his uniform.

Soon it began to rain. The drops fell faster and faster, till there was a heavy shower. When it was over, two boys walked by.

"Look," said one, "there is a tin soldier. He ought to have a boat to sail in."

So they made a boat out of paper, and they placed the tin soldier in it and sent him sailing down the gutter. The two boys ran alongside and clapped their hands. Large waves formed in the gutter, and the stream rolled on faster and faster! The rain had been very heavy indeed. The paper boat rocked up and down and turned around, sometimes so quickly that the tin soldier trembled. Yet he remained firm. His face did not change. He looked straight before him, rifle on his shoulder. Suddenly the boat shot under a bridge that formed a part of a drain, and then it became as dark as it had been in the tin soldier's box.

"Where am I going now?" he thought. "This is the goblin's fault, I am sure. If the little lady were only here with me in the boat, I would not care about the darkness."

Suddenly there appeared a great water rat who lived in the drain. "Have you a passport?" asked the rat. "Give it to me at once." But the tin soldier remained silent and held his rifle tighter than ever. The boat sailed on, with the rat following close behind, gnashing his teeth and crying out to the bits of wood and straw, "Stop him, stop him. He has not paid the toll, and he has not shown his passport!" But the stream rushed on stronger and stronger.

The tin soldier could already see daylight shining where the arch ended. Then he heard a roaring sound terrible enough to frighten even the bravest man. At the end of the tunnel the water fell over a steep drop into a large canal, which made it as dangerous for him as a waterfall would be for us. He was too close to it to stop, so the boat rushed on. The poor tin soldier could only hold himself as stiffly as possible, without moving an eyelid. That is how he showed he was not afraid.

The boat whirled around three or four times, and then it filled with water to the very top. Nothing could save it, and soon the tin soldier stood up to his neck in water. The paper became soft and loose, until at last it sank and the water closed over the soldier's head.

He thought of the little dancer whom he would never see again, and the words of a song sounded in his ears: "Farewell, warrior! ever brave, drifting onward to thy grave." Then the paper boat fell to pieces. Immediately after, the soldier was swallowed up by a great fish. Oh, how dark it was inside the fish—a great deal darker than inside the tunnel, and narrower, too. But the tin soldier held firm and lay at full length still shouldering his rifle.

The fish swam to and fro, making the most wonderful movements, but at last it became quite still. After a while, a flash of lightning seemed to pass through the fish, and then it was daylight. A voice cried out, "I have found a tin soldier!"

The fish had been caught, taken to the market, and sold to a cook, who took it into her kitchen and cut it open with a large knife. She picked up the soldier and held him by his waist between her finger and thumb, and then she carried him into a room.

Everyone was eager to see the wonderful soldier who had traveled inside a fish. He was placed on a table, and—how many curious things do happen in the world!—there he was in the very same room from whose window he had fallen. There were the same children and the same playthings standing on the table. There were his twenty-four brothers. There was the pretty castle with the elegant little dancer at the door. She still balanced herself on one leg and held up the other, just as firmly as he stood himself.

It touched the tin soldier so much to see her that he almost wept tin tears, but he kept them back. He only looked at her, and they both remained silent.

Suddenly one of the little boys took up the tin soldier and threw him into the fire. He had no reason for doing so. Perhaps it was the fault of the goblin who lived in the box.

The flames lighted the tin soldier as he stood. The heat was terrible, but whether it came from the real fire or from the fire of his love, he could not tell. Only then did he see that the bright colors of his uniform had faded. He did not know if they had been washed off during his journey or if they had faded from the effects of his sorrow.

He looked at the little dancer, and she looked at him. He felt himself melting away, but he still remained firm with his rifle on his shoulder. Suddenly the door to the room flew open, and a draft of air caught her up.

She fluttered right into the fire beside the tin soldier and was instantly in flames and then gone. The tin soldier melted down into a lump.

The next morning, when the maidservant took the ashes out of the stove, she found nothing resembling the little tin soldier. And of the dancer, nothing remained but the tinsel rose which, though blackened by the flames, was firmly affixed to a little tin heart.

The Nightingale

In China, as you know, the emperor is Chinese, and all those around him are Chinese, too. The story I am going to tell you happened to the emperor of China many years ago. That is all the more reason for telling it now, before it is forgotten.

This emperor lived in the most beautiful palace in the world. It was built entirely of porcelain and was decorated with gold and silver fabric.

In the garden were the most unusual flowers, each tied with pretty silver bells. Everyone who passed would stop to listen to the tinkling bells and admire the lovely flowers. Indeed, everything in the emperor's garden was remarkable. It extended so far that the gardener himself did not know where it ended. But those who traveled knew that beyond the palace grounds a noble forest with lofty trees sloped down to the deep blue sea. Great ships sailed under the shadows of these trees.

In one of the trees lived a nightingale who sang so beautifully that even the poor fishermen, who had many other things to do, would stop and listen. Sometimes, when they went at night to spread their nets, they would hear her sing and say, "Oh, how beautiful is the nightingale's song!"

Travelers from every country in the world came to the city of the emperor to admire the palace and gardens. But when they heard the nightingale, they all declared it the most wonderful of all. The travelers, on their return home, related what they had seen. Learned men wrote books that contained descriptions of the town, the palace, and the gardens. They did not forget to mention the nightingale, which they all agreed was really the greatest wonder. Those who could write poetry composed beautiful verses about the nightingale that lived in the forest near the deep blue sea.

The books traveled all over the world, and one of them came into the hands of the emperor. As he read he nodded his approval, for it pleased him to find such a beautiful description of his city, his palace, and his gardens. But when he came to the words, "The nightingale's song is the most beautiful of all," he exclaimed, "What is this? I know nothing of any nightingale. Is there such a bird in my empire? It is right in my garden and I have never heard it? It appears that even I have learned something from this book!"

Then he called one of his lords-in-waiting, who was so highbred that when someone of an inferior rank spoke to him or asked him a question, he would answer, "Pooh," which meant nothing.

"There is a very wonderful bird mentioned here called a nightingale," said the emperor. "I read that its song is the most wonderful thing in my kingdom. Why have I not been told of it?"

"I have never heard of this nightingale," replied the cavalier. "She has not been presented at court."

"It is my pleasure that she shall appear this evening," said the emperor. "It seems that the whole world knows what I possess better than I do myself."

"Though I have never heard of her," said the cavalier, "I will endeavor to find her."

But where was the nightingale to be found? The nobleman went up and down the stairs, through halls and passages. Yet no one he met had heard of the bird. So he returned to the emperor and said that the nightingale must be a fable, invented by the person who had written the book. "Your Imperial Majesty must not believe everything contained in books," he said. "Sometimes they are fiction."

"But the book in which I have read this account," said the emperor, "was sent to me by the great and mighty emperor of Japan. Therefore it cannot contain a falsehood. I shall hear the nightingale. She must be here this evening. If she does not come, the whole court will be punished after supper is ended."

"Tsing-pe!" cried the lord-in-waiting. Again he ran up and down the stairs and through all the halls and corridors. Half the court ran with him, for they did not like the idea of being punished after their supper. There was a great inquiry about this wonderful nightingale that all the world knew except those in the emperor's court.

At last they asked a poor little girl in the kitchen if she had ever heard of this bird. "Oh, yes," she said. "I know the nightingale quite well. Indeed, she sings most beautifully. Every evening I visit my poor sick mother who lives down by the seashore. I have permission to bring her scraps from the table. As I travel, I am often tired, and when I sit in the woods to rest, I listen to the nightingale's song."

"Little maiden," said the lord-in-waiting, "I will obtain constant employment for you in the kitchen, and you may bring a feast each night to your poor sick mother, if you will lead us to the nightingale, for she is invited this evening to the palace." So, with half the court behind her, the girl went into the woods where the nightingale sang. As they went along a cow began to low.

"Oh," said a young courtier, "now we have found her. What wonderful power for such a small creature."

"No, that is only a cow lowing," said the little girl with a laugh. "We are still a long way from the place."

Then some frogs began to croak in the marsh.

"Beautiful," said the young courtier again. "Now I hear it, tinkling like little church bells."

"No, those are frogs," said the little maiden. "But I think we shall hear her soon."

Presently the nightingale began to sing. "Hark, hark! There she sings," said the little maiden. "And there she sits," she added, pointing to a little bird perched upon a bough.

"Is it possible?" asked the lord-in-waiting. "I have never imagined the nightingale to be a little, plain, simple thing like that. She must certainly be impressed to see so many grand people around her."

"Little nightingale," called the girl, raising her voice, "our most gracious emperor wishes you to sing before him."

"With the greatest pleasure," answered the nightingale, who began to sing most delightfully.

"It sounds like tiny glass bells," said the lord-in-waiting. "And see how her little throat works. It is surprising that we have never heard this before. She will be a great success before the emperor."

"Did the emperor enjoy my song?" asked the nightingale, who thought he was present.

"My excellent little friend," said the courtier, "I have the great pleasure of inviting you to a court festival this evening, where you will sing before the emperor and gain imperial favor with your charming song."

"My song sounds best in the woods," said the bird. But she went willingly when she heard of the emperor's wish.

The palace was elegantly decorated for the occasion. The walls and floors of porcelain glittered in the light of a thousand lamps. Beautiful flowers with little silver bells stood in the corridors. A golden perch upon which the nightingale was to sit had been fixed in the center of the great hall. The whole court was present. The little kitchen maid, who was now installed as full court cook, had received permission to stand by the door. Everyone was in full dress, and every eye was turned to the little bird as the emperor nodded for her to begin.

The nightingale sang sweetly. Tears came into the emperor's eyes and rolled down his cheeks as her song became still more touching and went to everyone's heart. The emperor was so delighted he declared that the nightingale should be given a gold necklace to wear around her neck, but she declined the honor with thanks. She said that she had been sufficiently rewarded already.

"I have seen tears in my emperor's eyes," she said. "That is my richest reward. An emperor's tears have wonderful power and are quite sufficient honor for me." Then she sang again more enchantingly than ever.

"That singing is a lovely gift," said the ladies of the court to one another. Then they put water in their mouths to try to imitate the gurgling sounds of the nightingale whenever they spoke. And the footmen and the chambermaids also expressed their delight, which is saying a great deal, for they are very difficult to please.

In fact, the nightingale's visit was most successful. The emperor declared that she must live at court. She was given a golden cage and was permitted to go out twice each day and once each evening. Twelve servants were appointed to attend her on these occasions. Each held her by a silken string fastened to her leg, but there was certainly not much pleasure in this kind of flying.

The whole city spoke of the wonderful bird. Whenever two people met, one said "nightin," and the other said "gale," and they understood what was meant, for nothing else was spoken of. Eleven different peddlers named their children after her, but not one of them could sing a note.

One day the emperor received a large package on which was written THE NIGHTINGALE.

"Here no doubt is a new book about our celebrated bird," said the emperor. But instead of a book, it was a work of art—an artificial nightingale made to look like a living one. The bird was covered all over with diamonds, rubies, and sapphires. When the artificial bird was wound up, it could sing like the real one, moving its tail up and down. Around its neck hung a piece of ribbon on which was written THE EMPEROR OF CHINA'S NIGHTINGALE IS POOR COMPARED WITH THIS FROM THE EMPEROR OF JAPAN.

"It is very beautiful," exclaimed all who saw it. He who had brought the artificial bird received the title of "Imperial Nightingale-Bringer-in-Chief."

"Now they must sing together," said the court, "and what a duet it will be." But they did not get along well, for the real nightingale sang in its own natural way, but the artificial bird sang only one waltz.

"This is not a fault," said the music master. "To my taste, it is quite perfect." So then the artificial bird was made to sing alone, and was as successful as the real bird. Besides, it was so much prettier to look at, for it sparkled from its jewels. Thirty-three times it sang the same tune without being tired. The people would gladly have heard it again, but the emperor said the living nightingale should sing as well. But where was she? No one had noticed her when she flew out the window, back to her own green woods.

"What strange conduct," said the emperor when her flight had been discovered. All the courtiers blamed her and said she was a very ungrateful creature.

"But we have the best bird after all," said one. Then they had the bird sing again, although it was the thirty-fourth time they had listened to the same song. Even then they had not learned it, for it was rather difficult. The music master continued to praise the bird, even asserting that it was better than a real nightingale in both its dress and its musical power.

"For you must perceive, my chief lord and emperor, that with a real nightingale, we can never tell what is going to be sung. With this bird, everything is settled. It can be opened and explained, so that people may understand how the waltz is formed, and why one note follows after another."

"This is exactly what we think," they all replied. Then the music master received permission to exhibit the bird to the people of the empire on the following Sunday, so that they might hear it sing.

When they heard it, they were like people intoxicated. They all said "Oh!" and held up their forefingers and nodded. But one poor fisherman, who had heard the song of the real nightingale, said, "It sounds pretty enough. Yet there seems to be something wanting. I cannot tell exactly what."

After this, the real nightingale was banished from the empire. The artificial bird was placed on a silk cushion close to the emperor's bed. It was surrounded by presents of gold and precious stones. The artificial bird was even advanced to the title of "Little Imperial Singer."

The music master wrote all about the artificial bird. He filled twenty-five volumes with the most difficult Chinese words. Yet all the people claimed to have read and understood it, for they did not want the others to think they were stupid.

So a year passed, and the emperor, the court, and all the other Chinese knew every little turn in the artificial bird's song. For that reason, it pleased them even better. They could sing with the bird, which they often did. The

children on the street sang "Zi-zi-zi, cluck, cluck," and the emperor himself could sing it as well. It was really most amusing.

One evening, when the artificial bird was singing its best, and the emperor lay in bed listening to it, something inside the bird sounded "whizz." Then a spring cracked. "Whir-r-r-r" went all the wheels, running around, and then the music stopped.

The emperor immediately sprang out of bed and called for his physician. But he could do nothing. Then they sent for the watchmaker. After a great deal of talking and examination, the bird was put into something like a working order. But the watchmaker said that it must be used very carefully, since the barrels were very worn, and it would be impossible to put in new ones without injuring the music.

Now there was great sorrow, since the bird would only be allowed to play once a year. Even that was dangerous for the works inside it. But then the music master made a little speech, full of hard words, claiming that the bird was as good as ever, and of course no one contradicted him.

Five years passed, and then a real grief came upon the land. The Chinese were very fond of their emperor, and now he lay so ill that he was not expected to live. Already a new emperor had been chosen, and the people who stood in the street asked the lord-in-waiting about the old emperor.

"Pooh!" was his reply, and he shook his head.

Cold and pale, the emperor lay in his royal bed. Cloth had been laid down in the halls and passageways, so that not a footstep should be heard, and all was silent and still. The whole court thought the emperor was dead, so everyone ran away to pay homage to his successor. But the emperor was not yet dead, although he lay white and stiff on his bed.

A window stood open, and the moon shone in upon the emperor and his artificial bird. The poor emperor, finding he could scarcely breathe because of a strange weight on his chest, opened his eyes and saw Death beside him, wearing the emperor's golden crown and holding in one hand his sword of state and in the other his beautiful banner.

All around the bed peeping through the long velvet curtains were a number of strange faces. Some were very ugly, and others were lovely and gentle looking. These were the emperor's good and bad deeds, which stared him in the face now that Death sat at his heart.

"Do you remember this?" "Do you recollect that?" they asked one after another, thus bringing to his remembrance circumstances that made perspiration stand on his brow.

"I know nothing about it," said the emperor. "Music! music!" he cried. "Get me the large drum that I may not hear what they say." But still they went on, and Death nodded to all they said.

"Music! music!" shouted the emperor. "Oh, little precious golden bird, sing. Sing for me! I have given you jewels and costly presents. I have even hung

a golden necklace around your neck. Sing! sing!" But the bird remained silent. There was no one to wind it up, and therefore it could not sing a note.

Death continued to stare at the emperor with cold, hollow eyes, and the room was fearfully still. Suddenly there came through the open window the sound of sweet music. Outside, on the bough of a tree, sat the living nightingale. She had heard of the emperor's illness and had come to sing to him of hope and trust. As she sang the shadows grew paler and paler. The blood in the emperor's veins flowed more rapidly and gave life to his weak limbs. Even Death himself listened and said, "Go on, little nightingale. Sing on."

"If I sing more, will you give back the emperor's beautiful golden sword and that rich banner? Will you give back the emperor's crown?" asked the little bird.

Death gave up each of these treasures for a song. And the nightingale continued her singing. She sang of the quiet churchyard, where the white roses grow and the elder tree wafts its perfume on the breeze. She sang of the fresh, sweet grass moistened by the tears of the mourners. Then Death longed to go and see his garden. So he floated out through the window in the form of a cold, white mist.

"I thank you, most heavenly little bird. I know you well. I banished you from my kingdom once, and yet with your sweet song you have charmed away the evil faces from my bed and banished Death from my heart. How can I reward you?"

50

"You have already rewarded me," said the nightingale. "I shall never forget

that I drew tears from your eyes the first time I sang to you. These are the jewels that rejoice a singer's heart. But sleep now and regain your strength. I will sing to you again."

And as she sang the emperor fell into a sweet sleep. How mild and refreshing that slumber was! When he awoke, strengthened and restored, the sun shone brightly through the window. But not one of his servants had returned, since they all believed he was dead. Only the nightingale still sat beside him and sang.

"You must always remain with me," said the emperor. "You shall sing only when it pleases you. I will break the artificial bird into a thousand pieces."

"No, do not do that," replied the nightingale. "The bird did very well as long as it could. Keep it here still. I cannot build my nest and live in your palace. Let me come and go when I like. I will sit on a bough outside your window. In the evening, I will sing to you.

"I will fly far from you and your court to the homes of the fishermen and the peasants. Then I will come back and sing to you of those who are happy and of those who suffer, of the good and the evil in your kingdom. But you must promise me one thing."

"Anything," said the emperor, with the hand that held the heavy golden sword pressed to his heart.

"Let no one know that you have a little bird who tells you everything," she replied. "It will be best to conceal it." So saying, the nightingale flew away.

At last the servants came to look in on the dead emperor who, fully dressed in his imperial robes, stood and bid them good morning.

51

Thumbelina

here was once a woman who wished very much to have a child. After many years of waiting, she went to a fairy and said, "I should so very much like to have a little child. Can you tell me where I might find one?"

"Oh, that can be easily arranged," said the fairy. "Here is a barleycorn. It is different from the kind that grows in farmers' fields and is eaten by chickens. Put it into a flowerpot, and see what happens."

"Thank you," said the woman, and she took the barleycorn home and planted the seed. Immediately a large, handsome flower, something like a tulip in appearance, began to grow. Its red petals were tightly closed like a bud.

"What a beautiful flower," said the woman, and she bent to kiss the petals. As she did so, the flower opened. Within sat a very delicate and graceful little maiden. She was scarcely half as long as a thumb, so the woman named her Thumbelina.

Half a walnut shell, elegantly polished, served as Thumbelina's cradle. Her bed was made of the leaves of blue violets, and a rose petal was her cover. Here Thumbelina slept at night, but during the day she amused herself on a table, where the woman placed a plateful of water. Around this plate was a wreath of flowers, and on the water floated the petal of a tulip, in which Thumbelina sat and rowed from side to side with two oars made of white horsehair. It was a very pretty sight. While Thumbelina played, she would sing softly and sweetly. Nothing like her singing had ever been heard before.

One night a large, ugly toad crept through a broken pane of glass in the window and leaped upon the table where Thumbelina lay sleeping in her lovely bed.

"What a pretty little wife this would make for my son," said the toad, and she picked up the walnut shell in which Thumbelina lay. She carried it through the window and out into the garden to the swampy part of a broad stream where she lived with her son. The son was even uglier than his mother, and when he saw the pretty little maiden in her elegant bed, he cried out, "Croak, croak, croak."

"Don't speak so loudly, or you will awaken her," said the mother, "and then she might run away. Let us place her on one of the water-lily leaves out in the stream. It will be like an island to her. She is so light and small that she cannot escape. Then, while she is there, we will prepare a home under the marsh in which you two will live when you are married."

Far out in the stream grew a number of water lilies, with broad green leaves that seemed to float on the top of the water. The largest of these appeared farther off than the rest. So the old toad swam out to it, and there she placed the walnut shell in which Thumbelina was still sleeping.

Very early in the morning Thumbelina awoke and began to cry bitterly, for she knew she was very far from home. She could see nothing but water on every side of her and she knew there was no way of reaching the land.

Meanwhile, the old toad was very busy under the marsh, adorning the room with rushes and yellow wild flowers to make it look pretty for her new daughter-in-law. Then she swam with her ugly son to the leaf on which she had placed poor little Thumbelina. She wanted to fetch the pretty bed to put it in the bridal chamber.

The old toad bowed low in the water and said, "Here is my son. He will be your husband, and you will live happily in the marsh by the stream."

"Croak, croak, croak," was all the son could say for himself. So the old toad and her son took up the elegant little bed and swam away with it, leaving Thumbelina all alone on the green leaf where she sat and wept. She could not bear to think of living with the old toad and having her ugly son for a husband.

The little fishes who swam about in the water below had seen the old toad and heard what she said, so they lifted their heads above the water to look at the little maiden. As soon as they saw how pretty she was, it made them sorry to think of her having to live with the ugly toads.

"No, it must never be!" they said. So they joined together around the green stalk that held the leaf on which the tiny maiden stood. With their teeth they gnawed away until it was free. Then the leaf floated downstream, carrying Thumbelina far away.

As Thumbelina sailed past towns and villages, the little birds in the bushes saw her and sang, "What a lovely creature." The leaf floated farther and farther away with her, till at last she came to another land. Thumbelina was glad, for now the toads could not possibly reach her. The country through which she sailed was beautiful, and the sun shone upon the water till it glittered like liquid gold.

A graceful white butterfly fluttered around Thumbelina, and at last it alighted on the leaf. Thumbelina took off the sash she was wearing and tied one end of it around the butterfly. The other end she fastened to the leaf, which now glided much faster than ever, taking little Thumbelina with it.

Presently a large beetle flew by. The moment he caught sight of her, he seized Thumbelina around her delicate waist and flew with her into a tree. The green leaf floated away, the butterfly with it, for he was fastened to the leaf and could not get away.

Thumbelina felt frightened when the beetle flew with her to the tree, but she was especially sorry for the beautiful white butterfly she had fastened to the leaf. If he could not free himself, she knew he would die of hunger. But the beetle did not trouble himself at all about the matter. He seated himself by her side on a large green leaf, gave her some honey from the flowers to eat, and told her she was very pretty, though not in the least like a beetle.

After a time, other beetles gathered around. They turned up their feelers and one beetle said, "She has only two legs! How ugly that is!"

"She has no feelers," said another. "Her waist is quite slim. Pooh! She is like a human being."

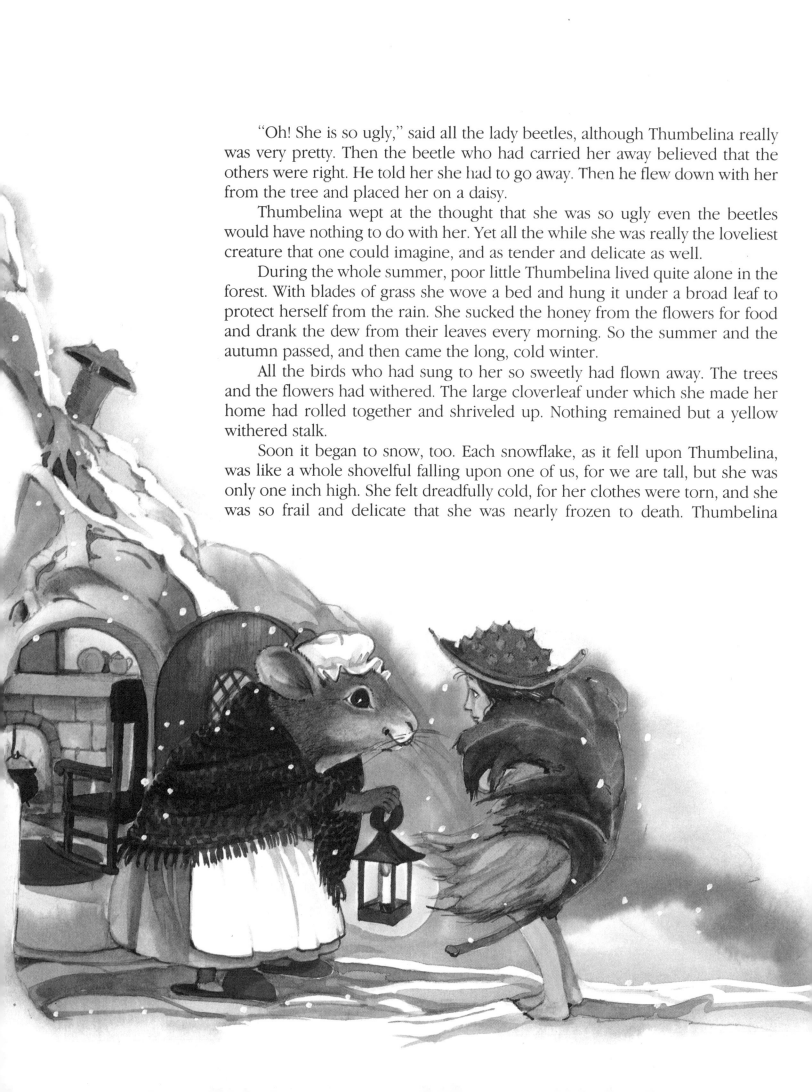

"Oh! She is so ugly," said all the lady beetles, although Thumbelina really was very pretty. Then the beetle who had carried her away believed that the others were right. He told her she had to go away. Then he flew down with her from the tree and placed her on a daisy.

Thumbelina wept at the thought that she was so ugly even the beetles would have nothing to do with her. Yet all the while she was really the loveliest creature that one could imagine, and as tender and delicate as well.

During the whole summer, poor little Thumbelina lived quite alone in the forest. With blades of grass she wove a bed and hung it under a broad leaf to protect herself from the rain. She sucked the honey from the flowers for food and drank the dew from their leaves every morning. So the summer and the autumn passed, and then came the long, cold winter.

All the birds who had sung to her so sweetly had flown away. The trees and the flowers had withered. The large cloverleaf under which she made her home had rolled together and shriveled up. Nothing remained but a yellow withered stalk.

Soon it began to snow, too. Each snowflake, as it fell upon Thumbelina, was like a whole shovelful falling upon one of us, for we are tall, but she was only one inch high. She felt dreadfully cold, for her clothes were torn, and she was so frail and delicate that she was nearly frozen to death. Thumbelina wrapped herself in a dry leaf, but it cracked in the middle and could not keep her warm. She shivered with the cold and would surely have frozen to death, had she not come upon the door of a field mouse, who had a little den in the cornfield. There the field mouse lived in warmth and comfort, with a kitchen, a beautiful dining room, and a whole roomful of corn. Poor little Thumbelina stood before the door just like a little beggar, asking for a small piece of corn, for she had been without a morsel to eat for more than two days.

"You poor little creature," said the field mouse. "Come into my warm home and dine with me." She was very pleased with Thumbelina, so she said, "You are quite welcome to stay with me all winter, if you like. But you must keep my rooms clean and neat and tell me stories, for I would like that very much."

Thumbelina did all the field mouse asked her and was quite comfortable.

"We shall have a visitor soon," said the field mouse. "My neighbor pays me a visit once a week. He is quite well off. He has large rooms and wears a beautiful black velvet coat. If you could only have him for a husband, you would be well provided for indeed. But he is blind, so please tell him some of your prettiest stories."

Thumbelina did not feel at all interested in this neighbor, for he was a mole. However, he came in his black velvet coat and paid his visit. He was rich and learned, no doubt, but he spoke poorly of the sun and the pretty flowers, because he had never seen them. Thumbelina sang to him, "Ladybird, ladybird, fly away home," and many other pretty songs. And the mole fell in love with her because she had such a sweet voice. But he said nothing, for he was very cautious.

A short time before, the mole had dug a long passage under the earth, leading from the dwelling of the field mouse to his own. He invited the field mouse and Thumbelina to walk with him through the passageway, but he warned them not to be alarmed at the sight of a dead bird that lay in the middle. It was a perfect bird, with a beak and feathers, and could not have been dead long.

The mole took a piece of phosphorescent wood that glowed like fire in the dark. Then he went before them to light their way through the long, dark passage. When they came to the spot where the dead bird lay, the mole pushed his broad nose through the ceiling. The earth gave way, and the daylight shone in through a large hole.

In the middle of the floor was a dead swallow, his beautiful wings pulled close to his sides. His feet and his head were drawn up under his feathers. The poor bird had evidently died of the cold. It made Thumbelina very sad to see him, she so loved the little birds. But the mole pushed it aside with his crooked legs and said, "He will sing no more. How miserable it must be to be born a bird! I am thankful that none of my children will ever be birds, for they can do nothing but cry 'Tweet, tweet,' and they always die of hunger in the winter."

"Yes, you may well say that!" exclaimed the field mouse. "What is the use

of his twittering, for when winter comes, he must either starve or be frozen to death. Still, birds are very highbred."

Thumbelina said nothing. When the two others had turned their backs on the bird, she leaned down and stroked the soft feathers that covered his face, and she kissed his closed eyelids.

"Perhaps you were the one who sang so sweetly to me in the summer," she said. "How much pleasure you gave me, you dear, pretty bird."

Then the mole stopped up the hole through which the daylight shone and accompanied the ladies home. But during the night, Thumbelina could not sleep. She got out of bed and wove a large, beautiful carpet of hay. She carried it to the dead bird and spread it over him, along with some down from the flowers she had found in the field mouse's room. The down was as soft as wool, and she spread some of it on each side of the bird so that he might lie warmly in the cold earth.

"Farewell, pretty bird," said Thumbelina. "Farewell, and thank you for your singing during the summer, when all the trees were green and the warm sun shone upon us." Then she laid her head upon the bird's breast, but she became alarmed. It seemed as if something inside the bird went *thump, thump.* It was the bird's heart! He was not really dead, only numbed by the cold. The warmth had revived him.

In autumn all the swallows fly away to warm countries, but if one happens to linger, the cold will seize it, and it becomes frozen, falling down as if dead. The swallow remains where it falls, and soon the cold snow covers it.

58

Thumbelina trembled. She was quite frightened, for the bird was large, a great deal larger than herself. But she took courage and laid the wool more thickly around the poor creature. Then she took a leaf she had used for her own blanket, and laid it over the bird's head.

The next morning, she again stole out to see him. The bird was alive but very weak. He could only open his eyes for a moment to look at Thumbelina, who stood holding a piece of the phosphorescent wood in her hand.

"Thank you, pretty little maiden," said the swallow. "I have been so nicely warmed that I shall soon be strong enough to fly again in the warm sunshine."

"Oh," she said. "It is cold out now. There is snow and freezing weather. Stay in your warm bed. I will take care of you."

Then she brought the swallow some water in a flower petal. The bird told her that he had hurt one of his wings on a thornbush, so he could not fly as fast as the other birds, who were soon far away on their journey to warm countries. At last he had fallen to the earth and could not remember how he came to be where Thumbelina had found him.

The swallow remained underground the whole winter, and Thumbelina nursed him with care and love. She told neither the mole nor the field mouse anything about it, for she knew they did not like swallows.

Before long springtime came, and the sun warmed the earth. It was time for the swallow to leave. Thumbelina opened the hole that the mole had made in the ceiling. The sun shone in upon them. The swallow asked Thumbelina to join him and fly away with him into the green woods. But Thumbelina knew that the field mouse would be very sad if she left her in this manner, so she said, "No, I cannot."

"Farewell, then, pretty little maiden," called the swallow as he flew out into the sunshine.

Thumbelina watched the bird go, and tears rose in her eyes. She had become very fond of him.

"Farewell," sang the swallow as he flew away into the green woods. Thumbelina felt very sad. She missed the warm sunshine and the world above the field mouse's home. But she was grateful to the field mouse and returned to her home, again saying not a word of her sorrow.

"You are to be married, Thumbelina," said the field mouse one day. "My neighbor, the mole, has asked for your hand. What good fortune for a poor child like you! Now we must prepare your wedding clothes. They will be made of both wool and linen. Nothing must be wanting when you are the mole's wife."

The field mouse hired four spiders to weave day and night, and Thumbelina was made to turn the spindle. Every evening the mole visited her. He spoke continually of the time when the summer would be over and they would celebrate their wedding day. For now the heat of the sun was so great that it burned the earth and made it quite hard. The mole looked forward to the time when the ground would become soft again.

As soon as the summer was over, the wedding was to take place. Thumbelina was not at all happy, for she did not like the tiresome mole. Every morning, when the sun rose, and every evening, when it went down, she would creep out the door. As the wind blew aside the ears of corn, she could see the blue sky. She thought how beautiful and bright it seemed out there, and she wished so much to see her dear swallow again. But he never returned, for by this time, he had flown far away into the lovely green forest.

When autumn arrived, Thumbelina had her outfit ready, and the field mouse said to her, "In four weeks the wedding will take place."

Then Thumbelina wept and said she could not marry the disagreeable mole.

"Nonsense," replied the field mouse. "Don't be troublesome, or I shall bite you with my teeth. He is a very handsome mole. The queen herself does not wear more beautiful velvets and furs. His kitchen and cellars are full. You should be very thankful for such good fortune."

So the day was set on which the mole was to fetch Thumbelina to live with him, deep under the earth. She would never again feel the sunshine, because he did not like it. Poor Thumbelina was very unhappy at the thought of saying good-bye to the beautiful sun, and since the field mouse had given her permission to stand at the door, she looked up at the sky one last time.

"Farewell," she cried, stretching out her arms toward the sun. Then she walked a short distance from the house. The corn had been cut, and only the dry stubble remained in the fields.

"Farewell, farewell," she repeated, twining her arm around a little red flower that grew just by her side. "Greet the little swallow for me, if you should see him again."

Just then she heard a sound. "Tweet, tweet," sounded above her head. Thumbelina looked up, and there was the swallow flying close by. When he saw Thumbelina, he was delighted. She told him how unwilling she was to marry the ugly mole and to live beneath the earth, never again seeing the bright sun. And as she told him she wept.

"Winter is coming," said the swallow. "I am about to fly away to warmer countries. Will you go with me? You can sit on my back. Fasten yourself on with your sash, and we can fly away from the ugly mole and his gloomy rooms—far away, over the mountains, to countries where the sun shines more brightly than here. There it is always summer, and the flowers bloom in great beauty. Fly now with me, dear little Thumbelina."

"Yes, I will go with you," said Thumbelina. And she seated herself on the bird's back and tied her sash to one of his strongest feathers.

Then the swallow rose in the air and flew over forests and seas, high above the snow-covered mountains. Thumbelina would have been frozen in the cold air, but she crept under the bird's warm feathers, keeping her little head uncovered so that she might see the beautiful lands over which they passed.

At last they reached the warm countries where the sun shone brightly and the sky seemed much higher above the earth. Lemons and oranges hung from trees in the woods. Beautiful children ran along the country lanes. Butterflies flitted about. As the swallow flew farther and farther, every place appeared more lovely than the last.

Finally they came to a blue lake. By the side of it, shaded by trees of the deepest green, stood a palace built of dazzling white marble. Vines clustered around its lofty pillars, and at the top were many swallows' nests. One of these belonged to the swallow who had carried Thumbelina.

"This is my home," he told her. "It will not do for you. You would not be comfortable. Choose one of those lovely flowers below, and I will put you down upon it. Then you will have everything you wish to make you happy."

"That will be delightful," Thumbelina said, and she clapped her hands for joy.

On the ground lay a large marble pillar that in falling had broken into three pieces. Between the pieces grew beautiful white flowers where Thumbelina chose to live. So the swallow flew down with her and placed her on one of the broad petals. How surprised she was to find, right in the middle of the flower, a tiny little man, as white and transparent as if he had been made of crystal. He had a gold crown on his head and delicate wings at his shoulders. He was not much larger than Thumbelina.

"Oh, how beautiful he is!" whispered Thumbelina to the swallow.

The little king was at first quite frightened of the bird, who was like a giant compared to a creature as tiny as himself. But when he saw Thumbelina, he was delighted, and he thought her the prettiest little maiden he had ever seen. He took the gold crown from his head and placed it on hers, asking Thumbelina to be his wife, and queen over all the flowers.

This was certainly a very different sort of husband from the son of the toad, or the mole with his black velvet jacket and fur. So she said yes to the handsome king. Then all the flowers opened, and out of each came a little lady or a tiny lord, all so pretty it was quite a pleasure to look at them.

Each of them brought Thumbelina a present. The best gift of all was a pair of beautiful wings that had belonged to a white butterfly. They were fastened to Thumbelina's shoulders so that she might fly from flower to flower.

Then there was much rejoicing, and the swallow, who sat above them in his nest, was asked to sing a wedding song, which he did as well as he could. But in his heart he felt sad, for he was very fond of Thumbelina and would have liked never to part from her again.

"You must not be called Thumbelina anymore," said the king of the flowers to her. "You are too pretty for such a name. We will call you Maia."

When winter was past, the swallow left the warm countries and flew to Denmark. "Farewell, farewell," he cried with a heavy heart. In Denmark he made a nest over the window of a house where a writer of fairy tales lived. The swallow sang "Tweet, tweet," and from his song came this story.

Great Claus and Little Claus

Once upon a time in a small village there lived two men with the very same name. Both were called Claus. One Claus was very rich and owned four horses. The other was poor and owned only one. So to tell them apart, people called the owner of the four horses "Great Claus." The one with just one was known as "Little Claus." This is the story of what happened to both of them.

For six days each week Little Claus plowed Great Claus's fields, using only his own one horse to do the work. But on the seventh day, Great Claus allowed Little Claus to use his four horses to do whatever he liked.

On Sundays, Little Claus would drive the horses through his field, pretending that all of the horses were his own. As the people going to church passed by in their very best clothing and carrying their prayer books, Little Claus would plow his fields, smacking his whip over the horses and calling out, "Gee-up, my five horses."

"You mustn't say that," Great Claus told him, "for only one of the horses is yours."

But Little Claus paid no attention to what Great Claus said he should and should not say. When anyone passed by, Little Claus continued to call out, "Gee-up, my five horses."

"I really must beg you not to say that again," said Great Claus. "If you do, I shall hit your horse on the head so that he will drop down dead on the spot. And then you will have no horse at all."

Little Claus agreed not to say it again, but as soon as the next person passed, he felt so proud to be seen plowing his field with five horses that he cried out, "Gee-up, my five horses!"

"I'll *gee-up* your horses for you," said Great Claus. And seizing a mallet, he struck Little Claus's one horse on the head, and it fell down dead.

"Now I have no horse at all," said Little Claus, weeping. But after a while he flayed the dead horse and hung the skin in the wind to dry. Then he put the dried skin into a bag, hung it over his shoulder, and went off to the next town to sell it. He traveled a great distance and had to pass through a dark and gloomy forest.

Presently a storm arose, and he lost his way. It was evening before Little Claus found the right path. He still had a long way to go before he reached the town, and it was too far to return home before nightfall. Near the road he saw a large farmhouse.

"Perhaps the people who live here will let me stay for the night," thought Little Claus, so he went up to the door and knocked.

The farmer's wife opened the door, but when she heard what Little Claus wanted, she told him to go away. Since her husband was not at home, she would not allow any strangers to stay.

"Then I shall have to sleep out here," said Little Claus to himself as the farmer's wife shut the door.

Close to the farmhouse stood a haystack, and between it and the house was a small shed with a thatched roof. "I can lie up there," said Little Claus, looking at the roof. "It will make an excellent bed."

So Little Claus climbed onto the roof of the shed. As he tossed about trying to make himself comfortable, he noticed that the wooden shutters of the farmhouse did not reach to the top of the windows. Through one of the openings Little Claus could see into the house, where a large table was set with wine, roast meat, and a splendid fish.

The farmer's wife and the parson from the church were sitting at the table together. Nobody else was there. The wife was filling the parson's glass with wine and helping him to large portions of fish and meat.

"If only I could have some too," thought Little Claus. Then he stretched out his neck toward the window and caught sight of a beautiful large cake. Indeed, there was a glorious feast before them.

At that moment he heard someone riding down the road toward the farm. It was the farmer coming home. This farmer was a good man, but he had one very strange prejudice—he could not bear the sight of the parson. If the farmer happened to see him, he would fly into a terrible rage. Because of this, the parson thought it best only to pay visits to the farmer's wife when her husband was away from home. The good woman was so thankful to the parson, she put before him the best of everything she had in the house to eat.

When they heard the farmer approaching, the two were terribly frightened. The woman told the parson to creep into a large chest that stood in the corner and hide. He did not resist, for he was well aware of how much the farmer disliked the sight of him. The woman then quickly hid all the fine food and the wine in the oven, because if her husband saw it, he would surely know that someone was there. Then she rushed to the door and let him in.

"Oh, dear," sighed Little Claus, who was watching from the roof and was sorry to see that all the food had disappeared.

"Is anyone up there?" asked the farmer, peering up at the shed to see who had spoken. The farmer looked right at Little Claus. "What are you doing up there? You must come down at once."

So Little Claus climbed down and went into the house. Then he told the farmer how he had lost his way, and asked if he might have shelter for the night.

"Certainly," said the farmer, "but first you must have something to eat."

The woman received them both very kindly, setting the table and serving each a large bowl of porridge. The farmer was hungry and ate heartily, but Little Claus was not fond of porridge and could not help thinking of the roast meat, the fish, and the cake, which he knew the wife had hidden in the oven.

Little Claus placed the sack in which he had put the hide of his horse on the floor by his feet. He stepped down on the sack and made the dried hide squeak quite loudly.

"Hush!" said Little Claus to his sack, at the same time treading on it again so that it squeaked louder than ever.

"What on earth have you got in your sack?" asked the farmer.

"Oh, it's a goblin," said Little Claus. "He says we needn't eat the porridge, for he has charmed the oven full of roast meat and fish and cake."

"What do you say?" asked the farmer, opening the oven door and seeing the nice things the woman had hidden, but which he thought the goblin had produced for them.

The woman dared not say anything, so she put the food before them, and they both had a hearty meal of fish and meat and cake.

Then Little Claus trod on the skin and made it squeak again.

"What does he say now?" asked the farmer.

"He says that he has also charmed three bottles of wine into the oven for us," Little Claus answered.

So the woman had to bring out the wine, too, and the farmer drank it and became very merry. The farmer very much wanted to have a goblin for himself, just like the one in Little Claus's sack!

"Can he charm out the devil?" asked the farmer. "I shouldn't mind seeing the devil just once, especially now that I am in such a merry mood."

"Oh, yes!" said Little Claus. "My goblin can do anything we ask." And he trampled on the sack till it squeaked louder than ever.

"He has agreed to do it," Little Claus said. "The goblin tells me that the devil will show himself in the image of your parson."

"Oh, dear!" said the farmer. "That's bad! I must tell you that I can't bear to see our parson. However, it doesn't matter. I'll know when I look at him that he is only the devil, and then I won't mind so much."

Little Claus then stepped down on the bag and put his ear close to it.

"What does he say?"

"He says you should open the chest in the corner. There you'll see the devil moping in the dark. But hold the lid tight so that he doesn't get out."

The farmer went straight to the chest where the woman had hidden the parson, who had heard everything that was said and was shivering with fright. The farmer lifted the lid slightly and peeped in.

"Ha!" he shrieked. "I saw him, and he looked exactly like our parson. It was a horrible sight!" The farmer had to have a drink after this. Then he and Little Claus continued drinking far into the night.

"You must sell me that goblin," said the farmer. "You may ask what you like for him! I'll give you a bushel of money."

"No, I can't do that," said Little Claus. "You must remember how useful my goblin is to me."

"Oh, but I must have him," said the farmer, and he went on begging.

"Well," said Little Claus at last, "since you have been so kind to me, I will give him up. You may have my goblin for a bushel of money, but I must have it full to the brim."

"That you will," said the farmer. "But you must also take that chest away with you! I won't have it in my house for another hour."

So Little Claus gave his sack with the dried hide in it to the farmer and received in return a bushel of money full to the brim. The farmer also gave him a large wheelbarrow in which to carry the money and the chest.

"Good-bye," said Little Claus, and off he went with his money and the big chest with the parson still in it.

On the far side of the woods was a river that was very deep and wide. The current in this river was so strong that it was almost impossible to swim against it. A large bridge stood across the river, and when Little Claus got into the middle of the bridge, he said in a voice that was loud enough for the parson to

hear, "What am I to do with this stupid old chest? It is so heavy, it must be full of large stones. I am quite tired of wheeling it along. Perhaps I'll just throw it into the river. If it floats to my house, well and good. If it doesn't, so be it."

Then he took hold of the chest and raised it up a bit, as if he were about to throw it into the water.

"No, no! Stop!" shouted the parson. "Let me out!"

"Help!" said Little Claus, pretending to be frightened. "The devil is still inside! Now I must certainly throw this chest into the river and drown him."

"Oh, no! Oh, no!" shouted the parson. "I am not the devil. I will give you a bushel of money if you let me out!"

"Well, that is another matter," said Little Claus, opening the chest. The parson crept out of the chest and pushed it into the water. Then he went home and gave Little Claus a whole bushelful of money. Now Little Claus had one bushel from the farmer and another from the parson, so his wheelbarrow was quite full of money.

"I got a pretty fair price for that horse, after all," he said to himself when he got back to his room and turned the money out of the wheelbarrow into a heap on the floor. "What a rage Great Claus will be in when he discovers how rich I have become through my one horse." So he sent a boy to borrow a bushel measure from Great Claus.

"What does he want that for?" wondered Great Claus. And he rubbed some fat on the bottom of the measure, so that a little of whatever was placed inside it would stick to the bottom. Indeed it did, for when the measure came back, there were three pieces of silver inside.

"What's this?" asked Great Claus, and he ran straight to Little Claus's home. "Where on earth did you get all this money?"

"Oh, this was payment for my horse's hide, which I sold last night."

"You were well paid indeed!" said Great Claus. And he ran home, took an axe, and hit all four of his horses on the head. He then flayed them and went off to town with the hides.

"Skins! Skins! Who will buy skins?" he shouted up and down the streets.

All the shoemakers and tanners in the town came running and asked him how much he wanted for the hides.

"A bushelful of money for each," said Great Claus.

"Are you mad?" they all asked. "Do you imagine we pay money by the bushel?"

"Skins! Skins! Who will buy skins?" he shouted again, and the shoemakers and the tanners became angry and drove Great Claus from the town.

"Little Claus will pay for this," he said when he got home. "I'll kill him for what he has done to me."

Meanwhile, at just this time, Little Claus's old grandmother died right in his house. Although she certainly had been very unkind to him, now that she was dead, he felt quite sorry about it. So Little Claus took the dead woman and put her into his warm bed to see if it could bring her back to life. He decided to leave her there for the night, while he slept on a chair in the corner.

As Little Claus sat in the dark, the door opened and in came Great Claus with his axe. He knew where Little Claus's bed stood, and he went straight to it and hit the dead grandmother on the forehead, thinking that it was Little Claus he had struck.

"Just see if you'll cheat me again after that," said Great Claus. Then he went home again.

"What a bad, wicked man he is," said Little Claus. "He was going to kill me. What a good thing that poor old granny was dead already!"

Then he dressed his old grandmother in her best Sunday clothes, borrowed a horse from his neighbor, and harnessed it to a cart. Little Claus set his grandmother on the back seat so that she would not fall out when the cart moved, and he started through the woods.

When the sun rose, Little Claus found himself outside a big inn. He stopped his horse and went inside to get something to eat. The landlord was a very, very rich man, and a good man, too, but he was known to have a terrible temper.

"Good morning," he said to Little Claus. "Why have you got your best clothes on so early in the morning?"

"I'm going to town with my old grandmother," said Little Claus. "She's sitting out there in the cart, and I can't get her to come in. Would you be so kind as to take a glass of water outside to her? You'll have to shout at her, though, for she's very hard of hearing."

"Of course," said the innkeeper, and he poured a large glass of water and took it out to the dead grandmother in the cart.

"Here is a glass of water," said the innkeeper. "Your grandson has sent it to you." The dead woman sat quite still and never said a word.

"Don't you hear me?" shouted the innkeeper. "I have brought you a glass of water from your grandson!" Again he shouted as loud as he could, and when she did not stir, he got angry and threw the glass of water in her face. The water ran all over her, and she fell backward out of the cart, for Little Claus had not tied her in.

"Now," shouted Little Claus as he rushed out of the inn and seized the landlord by the neck, "you have killed my old grandmother! Just look! There's a great hole in her forehead."

"Oh, what a misfortune!" exclaimed the innkeeper, clasping his hands. "That is the consequence of my fiery temper. Good Little Claus, I will give you a bushel of money and bury your grandmother as if she were my own if you will say nothing about this to anyone. Otherwise they will chop off my head, and that is so nasty."

So Little Claus got a whole bushel of money, and the innkeeper buried the grandmother just as if she had indeed been his own.

When Little Claus got home again with all his money, he immediately sent his boy over to Great Claus to borrow his measure.

"What?" said Great Claus. "Is he not dead? I shall have to see about this." So he, himself, took the measure over to Little Claus.

"I say, wherever did you get all this money?" he asked, his eyes round with amazement at what he saw.

"It was my grandmother you killed instead of me," said Little Claus. "I have sold her and got a bushel of money for her body."

"That was good pay indeed!" said Great Claus, and he hurried home, took an axe, and killed his own old grandmother.

He then put her in a cart and drove off to town. There he asked if the druggist would like to buy a dead body.

"Who is it, and where did the body come from?" asked the druggist.

"It is my grandmother. I have killed her for a bushel of money," said Great Claus.

"Heaven preserve us!" said the druggist. "You are talking like a madman. Please don't say such things. You might lose your head." And he pointed out what a horribly wicked thing Great Claus had done and how he deserved to be punished. Great Claus was so frightened that he rushed straight out of the shop, jumped into the cart, and galloped home.

"Little Claus shall pay for this!" shouted Great Claus when he got out of the town.

As soon as he got home, Great Claus took the biggest sack he could find, went over to Little Claus's house, and said, "You have deceived me again. First I killed my horses and then my old grandmother. It's all your fault, but you will not have another chance to cheat me!" Then he took Little Claus by the waist and threw him into the sack, put the sack on his back, and shouted, "I'm going to drown you!"

It was a long way to go before he came to the river, and Little Claus was not very light to carry. The road he was taking passed by a church in which an organ was playing and the people were singing beautifully. Great Claus put down the sack and went into the church.

"Oh, dear, oh, dear!" Little Claus sighed. He turned and twisted, but it was impossible to undo the cord. Just then an old cattle drover came along carrying a tall stick. He had a whole drove of cows and bulls before him. The animals bumped right into Little Claus's sack and upset it.

"Oh, dear," Little Claus sighed. "I am so young to be going to the Kingdom of Heaven!"

"And I," said the cattle drover, "am so old and still cannot get there!"

"Open the sack!" called Little Claus. "You may get in in place of me, and you will get to heaven directly."

"That will suit me just fine," said the cattle drover, undoing the sack for Little Claus, who immediately sprang out. "But you must promise to look after the cattle now," said the old man as he crept into the sack. Little Claus assured him he would and, tying up the top, walked off with the cattle.

A little while afterward, Great Claus came out of the church. Again he took the sack on his back and continued on his way to the river. There he threw in the sack with the old cattle drover inside it.

"Now you won't cheat me again!" he shouted, for he thought it was Little Claus he had drowned. Then he headed toward home. But when he reached the crossroads, he met Little Claus with the cattle.

"What is the meaning of this?" exclaimed Great Claus. "Did you not drown?"

"I did," said Little Claus.

"Then where did you get all these splendid beasts?" asked Great Claus.

"They are sea cattle," answered Little Claus. "I will tell you the whole story, and I thank you heartily for drowning me, for I am now a very rich man. I was very frightened when I was in the sack!" Little Claus told him. "The wind whistled in my ears when you threw me over the bridge into the cold water. I immediately sank to the bottom, but I was not hurt, for the grass is beautifully soft down there.

"The sack was opened by a beautiful maiden in snow-white clothes, wearing a green wreath in her wet hair. She took my hand and said, 'Welcome, Little Claus. Here are some cattle for you. A mile farther up the road you will come upon another herd, which I will give you too!'

"Then I saw that the river was a great highway for the sea folk. Down at the bottom they walked to and fro. The flowers were lovely, and the grass was so fresh! The fishes that swam about glided by just like birds in the air. How nice the people were, and what a lot of cattle strolled in the ditches!"

"Then why did you come straight up here?" asked Great Claus. "I shouldn't have done that if it was so fine down below."

"That's just my cunning," said Little Claus. "You remember I told you that the mermaid said that a mile farther up the road—and by the road she meant the river, for she can't go anywhere else—I should find another herd of cattle waiting for me. Well, I know how many bends there are in the river and what a roundabout way that would be. It is much shorter for me to cross the dry land and take the shortcuts. I can save time this way and get to the cattle that much sooner."

"Oh, you are a fortunate man," said Great Claus. "Do you think I could get some sea cattle if I were to go down to the bottom of the river?"

"I'm sure you would," said Little Claus. "But I can't carry you in a sack. You're too heavy for me. If you'd like to walk there and then get into the sack, it would be my pleasure to throw you into the river."

"Thank you," said Great Claus. "But if I don't get any sea cattle when I get down there, you can be sure you'll regret it when I return."

Then they walked back to the river together. As soon as the cattle saw the water, they rushed down to drink, for they were very thirsty. "See what a hurry they're in," said Little Claus. "They want to get down to the bottom again."

"You must help me first," said Great Claus. Then he crept into a big sack that had been lying across the back of one of the cows. "I'll put a big stone in, to be sure that I sink," said Great Claus.

"Oh, have no fear," said Little Claus as he gave the sack a push. *Plop!* went the sack, and Great Claus was in the river, where he sank to the bottom at once.

"I do fear he won't find any cattle," said Little Claus to himself as he drove home with his herd before him. And Great Claus learned once again that things are not always what they appear to be.

The Emperor's New Clothes

Many years ago there lived an emperor who was so fond of clothes that he spent all his money obtaining them. All he wanted was to be well dressed. He had a different suit of clothes for every hour of the day. This emperor did not care about his soldiers. The theater did not amuse him. In fact, the only thing he thought about was driving around his kingdom in a new suit of clothes.

The city where he lived was large and lively, with strangers arriving daily from all parts of the world. One day two men came to this city. They told everyone they were weavers and declared that they could weave the finest cloth imaginable. Their colors and patterns, they claimed, were not only exceptionally beautiful, but clothing made of their material possessed the extraordinary quality of being invisible to anyone who was unfit for his job or unpardonably stupid.

"That must be wonderful cloth," thought the emperor. "If I were to be dressed in a suit made of such cloth, I would be able to find out which people in my empire were unfit for their places, and I could tell the clever from the stupid. I must have some of this cloth woven for me without delay." So he gave a large sum of money to the weavers and told them to set to work at once.

The two men set up looms and pretended to be very hard at work. They asked for the finest silk and the most precious gold thread, but these they hid away in their bags and worked at the empty looms until late at night.

"I should very much like to know how they are progressing with the cloth," thought the emperor. But he felt rather uneasy when he remembered that anyone who was not fit for his office could not see the cloth. He was sure that he was, indeed, quite fit to be emperor, yet he thought it was better to send someone else first, just to see how the work was getting along.

"I shall send my honest old minister to see the weavers," thought the emperor. "He can judge best how the stuff looks, for he is intelligent, and nobody is more fit for his office than he."

The good old minister went into the room where the weavers sat pretending to be busy before the empty looms. "Heaven preserve us!" the minister thought, his eyes starting out of his head. "I cannot see anything at all!" But he was careful not to say so.

The weavers asked that he come nearer, pointing to the empty looms.

"Are the patterns not exquisite?" they asked. "Do you not find the colors beautiful?"

The poor old minister looked very hard, but he could see nothing, for there was nothing to be seen.

"Oh dear," he thought, "can I be so stupid? I should never have thought so. Is it possible that I am not fit for my office? No, I must not say that I am unable to see the cloth. Nobody must know!"

"Have you got nothing to say?" asked one of the weavers.

"Oh, it is very charming, exceedingly beautiful," replied the old minister, looking through his glasses. "What a beautiful pattern, what brilliant colors! I shall tell the emperor that I like the cloth very much."

"We are pleased to hear that," said the weavers as they went on to describe the colors and explain the curious pattern. The old minister listened attentively, so that he might relate to the emperor exactly what they said.

Then the weavers asked for more money, more silk, and more gold thread, which they said they required for their weaving. Again they kept everything for themselves. Not a thread came near their looms.

Soon afterward the emperor sent another honest courtier to the weavers to see how they were getting on and if the cloth was nearly finished. Like the old minister, the courtier looked and looked but could see nothing, since there was nothing to see.

"Is it not a handsome piece of cloth?" the two weavers asked the courtier, explaining to him the magnificent pattern that did not exist.

"I know I am not stupid," thought the man. "It must therefore be my good appointment for which I am not fit. I must not let anyone know." And he praised the cloth, which he could not see, and he expressed his admiration for the beautiful colors and the fine pattern. "It is excellent," he told the emperor.

Everybody in the city talked about the remarkable quality the fabric possessed. All were anxious not to appear unfit or stupid. And at last the emperor wished to see the cloth for himself. With a number of courtiers, including the two who had been there before, he went to the two weavers, who were now working as hard as they could, but still without using any thread.

"Is it not magnificent?" asked the two old statesmen. "Your Majesty must admire both the colors and the pattern." And then they pointed to the empty looms, for they imagined the others could see the cloth.

"What is this?" said the emperor to himself. "I do not see anything at all. This is terrible! Am I stupid? Am I unfit to be emperor? That would indeed be the most dreadful thing that could happen to me.

"Really," he said, turning to the weavers, "your cloth has our most gracious approval." Nodding contentedly, he looked at the empty loom, for he would not say that he saw nothing at all. All the attendants who were with him looked and looked, and though none could see any more than the others, they agreed it was very beautiful. All advised the emperor to have his handsome new fabric made into a suit of clothes to wear at the great procession that was soon to take place.

"It is magnificent, beautiful, excellent," everyone said, and they all seemed delighted. The emperor appointed the two men imperial court weavers.

The whole night before the day of the procession, the weavers pretended to work, burning more than sixteen candles. People could see that they were busy finishing the emperor's new suit. Pretending to take the cloth from the loom, they worked in the air with big scissors and sewed with needles without thread. At last they said, "The emperor's new suit is ready."

The emperor and all his barons then came to the hall. The weavers held their arms up as if there were something in their hands and said, "Here are the trousers! This is the coat! Here is the cloak!" And so on. "They are each as light as a cobweb, and you will feel as if you have nothing at all upon your body. That is the beauty of them."

"Indeed!" said all the courtiers. But they could see nothing, for, in fact, there was nothing to be seen.

"Does it please Your Majesty now to graciously undress?" asked the weavers. "Then we may assist you in putting on your new suit."

The emperor undressed, and the weavers pretended to hand him each of the new garments they were supposed to have made. Then they held him at the waist as if they were fastening on the train. The emperor looked at himself from every side in the mirror.

"How well they suit Your Majesty! What a wonderful fit!" said everyone. "What a beautiful pattern! What fine colors! What a magnificent suit of clothes!"

The master of ceremonies announced that the bearers of the canopy, which was to be carried in the procession, were ready.

"I too am ready," said the emperor. "Does not my suit fit me marvelously?" Then he turned once more to the mirror, so that people should think he was admiring his garments.

The chamberlains, who were to carry the train, stretched their hands to the ground, groping as if they were lifting up a train and pretending to hold it in their hands. They did not want people to know that they could not see anything.

The emperor marched in the procession under the beautiful canopy, and everyone who saw him exclaimed, "Indeed, the emperor's new suit is the finest he has ever had! What a long train! How well it fits him!" Nobody wished to let

the others know he saw nothing, for then he would have been thought stupid or unfit for his office. Never were the emperor's clothes more admired.

Suddenly a child in the crowd spoke the truth. "He has nothing on at all," he said.

"Good heavens! Listen to the voice of a child," said the father, and one person whispered to the next what the child had said. And then all the people cried out together, "But the emperor has nothing on at all."

That made a deep impression upon the emperor, for it seemed to him that they were right. But he thought to himself, "Now I must bear up to the end." And he walked on with great dignity as the chamberlains carried the train that was not there.

The Fir Tree

Deep in the forest where the sun is warm and the air is fresh grew a fir tree. Yet this pretty little fir tree was not happy. It wished so much to be tall like its companions, the pines and firs that grew around it.

The sun shone down on the little fir tree. The soft air fluttered its leaves. The little peasant children passed by, chattering merrily. But the fir tree paid no attention.

Sometimes the children would bring large baskets of raspberries or strawberries and would sit near the fir tree and say, "This little tree is the prettiest." This made the fir tree feel even more unhappy than before, so sorry was it to be little.

All the while the tree kept growing a notch or joint taller. As it grew, it complained, "Oh! How I wish I were as tall as the other trees. Then I would spread out my branches on every side, and my top would overlook the wide world. The birds would build their nests on my boughs, and when the wind blew, I would bow with stately dignity like my tall companions."

The tree was so discontented that it took no pleasure in the warm sunshine, the birds, or the rosy clouds that floated over it morning and evening. Sometimes, in winter, when the snow lay white and glittering on the ground, a hare would come springing along and jump right over the little tree. How mortified it would feel!

Two winters passed, and when the third arrived, the tree had grown so tall that the hare had to run around it. Still the tree remained unsatisfied and would exclaim, "Oh, if I could just keep on growing tall and old! There is nothing else worth caring for in the world!"

That autumn, as usual, the woodcutters came and cut down several of the tallest trees. The young fir tree, which had now grown very tall, shuddered as the noble trees fell to the earth with a crash. After the branches were lopped off, the trunks looked so slender and bare that they could scarcely be recognized. Then they were placed upon wagons and drawn out of the forest by horses.

"Where are they going? What will become of them?" The young fir tree wished very much to know. So in the spring, when the swallows and the storks came, it asked, "Do you know where those trees were taken? Did you meet them?"

The swallows knew nothing, but one stork, after a little reflection, nodded his head and said, "Yes, I think I do. I met several new ships when I flew from Egypt, and they had fine masts that smelled like fir. I think these must have been made from the trees. I assure you they were stately, very stately indeed."

"Oh, how I wish I were tall enough to go to sea," said the fir tree. "What is the sea? What does it look like?"

"It would take too much time to explain," said the stork, flying away quickly.

"Rejoice in your youth," said the sunbeam. "Rejoice in your fresh growth and young life," the wind said, and kissed the young tree as the dew watered it with tears. But the fir tree paid no attention to them at all.

Christmastime drew near, and many young trees were cut down. Some were even smaller and younger than the fir tree, who so longed to leave its forest home. These young trees, which were chosen for their beauty, kept their branches. They too were laid on horse-drawn wagons and carried out of the forest.

"Where are they going?" asked the fir tree. "They are not taller than I. Indeed, one is much smaller. And why are their branches not cut off?"

"We know, we know," sang the sparrows. "We have looked in the windows of the houses in the town. We know what becomes of them. They are dressed up in the most splendid manner. We have seen them standing in the middle of a warm room, adorned with honey cakes, gilded apples, playthings, and many hundreds of wax tapers."

"And then," asked the fir tree, trembling through all its branches, "and then what happens to them?"

"We did not see any more," said the sparrows. "That was enough for us."

"I wonder whether anything so brilliant will ever happen to me," thought the fir tree. "It would be much better than crossing the sea. Oh! When will Christmas be here again? I am now as tall and well grown as those who were taken away last year. Oh, that I were now laid on the wagon, or standing in the warm room with all that brightness and splendor around me! Something better and even more beautiful must come after what the sparrows saw, or the trees would not be so decked out. Yes, what follows must be grander and even more splendid. What can it be? I am weary with longing."

"Rejoice with us," said the air and the sunlight. "Enjoy your life in the fresh air."

But the tree would not rejoice, though it grew taller every day. Throughout the winter and summer, its dark-green foliage might be seen in the forest. Passersby would say, "What a beautiful tree!"

A short time before Christmas, the men with the wagons arrived. The fir tree was the first to be cut down. As the axe cut through its stem, the tree fell with a groan to the earth, conscious only of pain and faintness. Its sorrow at leaving its home in the forest was so great that the fir tree forgot how much it had looked forward to this happiness. The tree knew that it would never again see its dear old companions, the trees, nor the little bushes and many-colored flowers that had grown by its side. Perhaps it would never again see the birds as well.

The journey was most unpleasant. The tree had barely recovered when it, along with several other trees, was unloaded in the courtyard of a house. The first words it heard came from a man, who said, "We only want one, and this is the prettiest."

Then two servants came and carried the fir tree into a large and beautiful home. On the walls hung pictures. Near the great stove stood china vases with lions on the lids. There were rocking chairs, silken sofas, large tables covered with pictures and books, and playthings were all about the floor.

Then the fir tree was placed in a large tub full of sand, which was covered with lovely green felt. The tub itself stood on a very handsome carpet. How the fir tree trembled! What was going to happen now? It barely had time to wonder when some young ladies arrived, and the servants helped them decorate the tree. On one branch they hung little bags cut out of colored paper. Each bag was filled with candies. On others they hung gilded apples and walnuts, as if they had grown there. All around were hundreds of red, blue, and white tapers, which were fastened onto the branches. Dolls exactly like real babies were placed under the green leaves. At the very top was fastened a glittering star made of tinsel. Oh, it was very beautiful!

"This evening," they all exclaimed, "how bright it will be!"

"Oh, that the evening were here," thought the tree, "and the tapers lighted! Then I shall know what else is going to happen to me. Will the trees of the forest come to see me? I wonder if the sparrows will peep in the windows as they fly by? Shall I grow here in this tub, wearing all these ornaments throughout the year?"

But guessing was of very little use. It made the tree's bark ache, and this pain is as unpleasant for a slender fir tree as a headache is for us. At last the tapers were lighted, and then what a glow of light the tree presented! It so trembled with joy in all its branches that one of the candles fell among the green leaves and burned some of them.

"Help! Help!" exclaimed the young ladies, but there was no danger, for they quickly extinguished the fire. After this, the tree tried not to hurt any of the beautiful ornaments, even though it was overwhelmed by their brilliancy.

Suddenly the folding doors to the room were thrown open, and a troop of children rushed in. First they were silent with astonishment. Then they shouted for joy. The room rang with their merriment. They danced gaily around the tree, while one treat after another was taken from it. "What are they doing? What will happen next?" wondered the fir tree.

At last the candles burned down to the branches and were put out. Then the children were given permission to plunder the tree. Oh, how they rushed upon it, till some of the branches cracked. Had the tree not been fastened with the glistening star to the ceiling, it would have fallen to the floor. The children then danced about with their pretty toys, and everyone forgot about the tree, except the children's maid, who came and peeped among the branches to see if an apple or a fig had been forgotten.

"A story, a story," cried the children, pulling a little old man toward them.

"Now we shall sit in the shade," the man said, laughing as he seated himself beneath the tree. "I shall only tell one story," he said. "What shall it be?"

The children called this name and that, and there was a great deal of shouting and crying out. At last it was decided that "Humpty Dumpty" was the favorite. The fir tree remained quite still and thought to itself, "Shall I have anything to do with all this?" But the tree had already amused the children as much as they wished.

The old man began the story of Humpty Dumpty—how he fell off the wall and was raised again and married a princess. The children sat quietly and listened. When it was over they clapped their hands and cried, "Tell another, tell another." But the man would not.

After this, the fir tree became quite silent and thoughtful. Never had the birds in the forest told such a tale as "Humpty Dumpty."

"Ah, yes, so this is how it is in the world," thought the fir tree. It believed the whole story because it was told by such a nice man.

"Well," the fir tree thought, "who knows? Perhaps I may fall down too, and then I may marry a princess." The fir tree looked forward to the next evening, expecting to be decorated again with lights and playthings, gold and fruit.

"Tomorrow I will not tremble," it thought. "I will enjoy all my splendor. I shall hear a story again, as well." And the tree remained quiet and thoughtful all night. In the morning the servants and the housemaid came in.

"Now," thought the fir tree, "all my splendor is going to begin again." But to its surprise, it was dragged out of the room and up the stairs to the garret. There the tree was thrown on the floor in a dark corner where no daylight shone. And there it was left.

"What does this mean?" thought the tree. "What am I to do here? I can hear and see nothing in a place like this." The fir tree had plenty of time to think. Days and nights passed, and no one came near it. When at last somebody did come, it was only to put away some large boxes in a corner. So the tree was completely hidden from sight, as if it had never existed.

"It is winter now," thought the tree. "The ground is hard and covered with snow, so no one can plant me. I suppose I shall be sheltered here until spring comes. How thoughtful and kind the people are to me! Still, I wish this place was not so dark and lonely, with not even a little hare to look at. How pleasant it was in the forest, when the snow lay on the ground and a hare would run by. Yes, and jump over me, too. Although I did not like it then. Oh! It is terribly lonely here."

"Squeak, squeak," said a little mouse, creeping cautiously toward the tree. Then came another, and both of them sniffed at the fir tree and crept between its branches.

"Oh, it is very cold," said the little mouse. "If it were not, we would be quite comfortable here, wouldn't we, old fir tree?"

"I am not old," said the fir tree. "There are many who are older than I."

"Where do you come from? What do you know?" asked the mice, who were full of curiosity. "Have you seen the most beautiful places in the world? Can you tell us all about them? Have you been in the storeroom where cheeses lie on the shelves and hams hang from the ceiling? There you go in thin and come out fat."

"I know nothing of that place," said the fir tree. "But I know the woods where the sun shines and the birds sing." And then the tree told the little mice all about its youth. They had never heard such an account in their lives. After they had listened attentively, they said, "What a number of things you have seen! You must have been very happy."

"Happy!" exclaimed the fir tree, and then, as it reflected upon what it had

been telling the mice, it said, "Ah, yes! After all, those were happy days." And then it went on and related all about Christmas Eve, and how it had been dressed up with candies and apples and lights. The mice said, "How happy you must have been, old fir tree."

"I am not old at all," replied the tree. "I only came from the forest this winter. I am now checked in my growth."

"What splendid stories you tell," said the little mice. The next night, four other mice came with them to hear what the tree had to tell. The more it talked, the more it remembered, and then it thought, "Those were happy days, but they may come again. After all, Humpty Dumpty fell off the wall, and yet he married the princess in the end. Perhaps I will marry a princess too." Then the tree remembered a pretty little birch tree that grew in the forest, which was, to the fir tree, a beautiful princess indeed.

"Who is Humpty Dumpty?" asked the little mice. And then the tree related the whole story. He could remember every single word, and the little mice were so delighted with it that they were ready to jump to the top of the tree.

The next night a great many more mice made their appearance. On Sunday two rats came, too. But they said that "Humpty Dumpty" was not a pretty story at all, and the little mice were very sorry, for it made them think less of it.

"Do you know only one story?" asked the rats.

"Only one," replied the fir tree. "I heard it on the happiest evening of my life. But I did not know I was so happy at the time."

"We think it is a miserable story," said the rats. "Don't you know a story about bacon in the storeroom?"

"No," replied the tree.

"Many thanks to you, then," replied the rats, and off they marched.

The little mice also kept away after this, and the tree sighed and said, "It was very pleasant when the merry little mice sat around me and listened while I talked. Now that has passed too. However, I shall consider myself happy when someone comes to take me out of this place."

But would that ever happen? Yes! One morning some people came to clear out the garret. The boxes were packed away, and the tree was pulled from the corner and dragged roughly out upon the staircase, where the daylight shone.

"Life is beginning again," said the tree, rejoicing in the sunshine and fresh air. Then it was carried downstairs and taken into the courtyard so quickly that it forgot to think of itself and could only look about. There was much to be seen. The courtyard was close to a garden, where flowers and trees were blooming. Fresh and fragrant roses hung over the little palings. The swallows flew here and there, crying, "Twit, twit, twit, my mate is coming." But it was not the fir tree they meant.

"Now I shall live," cried the tree, joyfully spreading out its branches. But alas! Its branches were all withered and yellow, and the fir tree lay in a corner among weeds and nettles. The star of gold tinsel still stuck in the top of the tree, glittering in the sunshine.

In the courtyard two of the merry children who had danced around the tree at Christmas were playing. The youngest saw the gilded star and pulled it off the tree.

"Look what is sticking to the ugly old fir tree," said the child, treading on the branches till they crackled under his boots. The fir tree saw all the fresh bright flowers in the garden, and then looked at itself, wishing it had remained hidden in the dark corner of the garret.

It thought of its youth in the forest, of the merry Christmas evening, and of the little mice who had listened to the story of Humpty Dumpty.

"Past! Past!" said the old tree. "Oh, had I but enjoyed myself while I could have done so! But now it is too late." Then a lad came and chopped the tree into small pieces, throwing them into a heap on the ground. The pieces were placed in a fire under the pot, and they quickly blazed up brightly, while the tree sighed so deeply that each sigh was like a pistol shot.

Then the children, who were at play, came and sat in front of the fire and looked at it and cried, "Pop, pop!" along with the tree. But each "pop" that the tree made was really a sigh. The tree was thinking of the summer days in the forest, of Christmas evening, and of Humpty Dumpty, the only story it had ever heard or knew how to relate, till at last it was consumed.

The boys went back to play in the garden, the youngest still wearing on his breast the golden star the tree had worn during the happiest evening of its life. Now all was past. The tree's life was past, and this story, also. For, at last, all stories must come to an end.

The Princess and the Pea

Once upon a time there was a prince who wanted to marry a princess. But she had to be a real princess in every way. He traveled all over the world, but nowhere could he find what he wanted. Everywhere he went there were women who claimed they were real princesses, but it was difficult to find one he believed was truly a princess in every way. There was always something about each one that was not as it should be. So he came home again and was sad, for marrying a real princess was very important to him.

One evening there was a terrible storm. There was thunder and lightning, and the rain poured down in torrents. Suddenly a knocking was heard at the castle gate, and the old king went to open it.

There stood a princess in front of the gate. But good gracious! What a sight the rain and the wind had made of her good looks. The water ran down from her hair and clothes. It ran down into the heels of her shoes and out again at the toes. And yet she said that she was a princess nonetheless.

She was brought into the palace and given dry clothing to wear and food to eat. The prince was quite pleased when he saw how pretty she was. But how could he be sure she was indeed a real princess?

"Well, we'll soon find that out," thought the old queen when she heard what was happening. But she said nothing. Quietly she slipped into the guest room and took all the bedding off the bedstead. Then she placed a pea on the bottom. Next she took twenty mattresses and laid them on the pea, and then twenty feather comforters on top of the mattresses.

On this the princess had to lie all night. In the morning she was asked how she had slept.

"Oh, very badly!" she said. "I scarcely closed my eyes all night. Heaven only knows what was in the bed, but I was lying on something so hard that I am black and blue all over my body."

The old queen knew at once that the princess was a real princess because she had felt the pea right through the twenty mattresses and the twenty feather comforters. Nobody but a real princess could be as sensitive as that. So the prince took her for his wife, and the pea was put in the museum, where it may still be seen, if no one has stolen it.